FIAMMETTA

FIAMMETTA

NORA BECK

CARLTON STREET PRESS
Portland, Oregon

CARLTON STREET PRESS
P.O. Box 82212
Portland, OR 97282-0212

www.carltonstreetpress.com

Book design by Alice Martin Design & Illustration

Beck, Nora.
Fiammetta / Nora Beck
ISBN 0-971-28250-1 (Hard Cover)
ISBN 0-971-28251-X (Soft Cover)

"Uncle Riccardo's Driving Lesson,"
2001 copyright © Nora Beck.
First published in *The Oregon Review*.

"Two Topless Girls on the Beach,"
1999 copyright © Nora Beck.
First published in *Phoebe:
Journal of Feminist Scholarship, Theory, and Aesthetics*.

"The Good Witches of Porciano,"
2002 copyright © Nora Beck.
First published in *The Artisan Magazine*.

"The artist (sister),"
1999 copyright © Nora Beck.
First published in *Synergia*.

Printed and bound by Ash Creek Press

For Liz, whose warmth, generosity, and
beauty inspire me.

Acknowledgements

I am grateful to friends who have supported me through
the years, including Margo Ballantyne, Steven Bernstein, Gabriel
Blumenthal, Jacob Blumer, Kacia and Clark Brockman, Ann
Christensen, Joy Collman, Janet Davidson, Annie Dawid, Dinah
Dodds, Kathy Emery, Fiorenza Gilioli, Elena Furin, Courtney
Goodmonsen, Andrew Holder, Danny Koch, Amy Lavine, Matthew
Levinger, Eric Lundgren, Wendy McLennan, Judy McMullen, Livia
Nicolescu, Dawn Norfleet, Rachel Ostroy, Marianna Ritchey, Peggy
Rielly, Elaine Sisman, Constance and John Strawn, Harriet Wingard,
and Lora Worden.

I wish to show my appreciation to my Aunt Becki, Ned
Rorem, Meredith Monk, my parents, Darma and James, and brother,
Lawrence, for a lifetime of stories.

Thank you to Paul Merchant for editing the manuscript and making
valuable suggestions and to Jill Teasley for her thoughtful copyedit-
ing and unwavering enthusiasm for my work.

I reserve a special debt of gratitude to the wonderful and amazing
Alice Martin, who designed the book's cover and layout.

FIAMMETTA

I like to tell stories, and some of them have even happened to me.

She had two affairs during her New York sojourn. The first happened Wednesday with Mary, the surfer. They had been seeing each
other on and off for two weeks before taking the big plunge. After a
night at the Hong Kong Movie Theater in Chinatown, Mary invited
Fiammetta over to her apartment for the evening-ending cup of tea,
which turned into just the beginning. While Fiammetta was inno-
cently sipping her chamomile brew, Mary caressed her hand.
Fiammetta finally put the cup down and Mary led her to the bedroom and shut the door to keep the cats out. Fiammetta is allergic to
cats, a dilemma for any lesbian in search of a night of fun.

The next affair involved cats too. Two of them. The cats followed
Fiammetta and Foxie, the English nurse with blue hair, Friday
night. After her dinner party, which featured fish and chips, Foxie

took Fiammetta to her building's roof.

"Do you like to look at the stars, Foxie?"

"Doesn't everyone?" she answered, putting her arm around Fiammetta's waist. "Let's sit down."

"Great spot, really," Fiammetta uttered her last words before being inundated by Foxie's slippery kisses. After about fifteen minutes, Foxie led her down to her apartment, scattered the cats from her room, and lit a candle. Fiammetta left the next morning at around noon with just enough time to pack her bags for Italy.

Simon and Jennifer got married three years ago. It was love at first sight in the introductory macroeconomics class at Harvard Business School. Jennifer sat dutifully in the front row, notebook open, pen in hand, looking nervous. Simon sat in the back, chewing gum, asking his neighbor for a pen, and writing notes on the back of his bank statement. After class they bumped into each other as Jennifer scrambled for the door. Simon dropped his book bag on her feet.

"I'm really sorry," he said.

"Don't worry about it."

They have never been apart much since. He calmed her down and she revved him up. They worked on all the case studies together, exchanged ideas, made love, and exchanged more ideas. They didn't make any other friends that first year. And for all their trouble, they pulled A's in every course. It was no *Paper Chase* either. Her father wasn't a professor at Harvard and he was not the son of some middle-class worker bee. They both attended very good private schools and had doctors for fathers: Simon's was a neurosurgeon who verbally attacked his children, Jennifer's a thoracic surgeon who had boyfriends on the side. Both had mothers who tagged along at slushy doctors' drinking parties.

After graduate school, Simon and Jennifer moved to New York City to make their fortune. Simon got a job working for Chase Manhattan in its pension funds division. He started as the vice president of his group, skipping over other people in line for the position, people who had worked there for ten years but who did not have the Harvard degree. At first, his underlings resented him, but once they really got to know him, they learned to like him. He was really a pretty honest and good guy.

As for Jennifer, she decided to pursue a more artistic route, landing a job as assistant to an art dealer. She managed his office while learning the business of buying and selling art. She'd majored in art history at college and enjoyed painting landscapes before succumbing to her father's pressure to follow a more lucrative career, like business. ("You'll never make a steady living making art.") She felt comfortable in her office, surrounded by various objets d'art, a Picasso print and a painting by Helen Frankenthaler. In the evenings they returned to their Upper West Side apartment, ordered in Chinese food, watched television, or rented a video.

They smiled at each other tons and one day decided to get married. That Wednesday they took the day off, and with rings in hand, skipped down to the justice of the peace at City Hall. From pay phones they called their respective families collect and told them of the blessed event. Their families were happy and not surprised by their decision. Simon and Jennifer were meant for each other, after all. They joined the legion of newlyweds who crawled around New York City, spending their money at Zabar's and Macy's and seeing trendy foreign movies in Greenwich Village. Life was good, but not particularly examined.

Fiammetta's flight arrived in Pisa at 11:00 A.M. The airport resembled the small shopping mall in Kingston, New York, where she used to purchase cheap lamps and other assorted home furnishings. After lifting her bag off the conveyor belt, she made her way to the Hertz counter to pick up the rental car. The people organizing the conference said they would pay for her flight, put her up in a nice hotel, and throw in the car. How else was she supposed to get to Cennina, a small medieval town perched in the Tuscan hills?

The man behind the counter looked slightly counter-culture for Italy: he wore a sweatshirt and blue-tinted sunglasses.

"Your name?" he asked in a pretty good English accent.

"Stern," she replied in a voice that had spent the last six hours sleeping sitting-up. He rapidly punched numbers into the computer. Then the most annoying family with two screaming kids crawled up behind her and, in typically Italian fashion, the father put one kid on the counter right next to Fiammetta's forearm. Italians wait in line a grappolo d'uva, like a bunch of grapes.

The hip Hertz guy forked over the keys to a subcompact Fiat and told her that it was the white one in parking spot number 15. She thanked him for his expedience, and after one last grimace aimed at the Italian father, picked up her Coach bag, sensibly packed, and marched out toward the car. Fiammetta was trying to unlearn her impatience now that she lived in Reno. Her father had picked her up at Kennedy Airport last Christmas and became verbally caustic while waiting to pay the parking fee. Uncomfortable with his nervous energy, Fiammetta said, "Dad, we'll get there when we get there." He replied, "I see you are no longer a New Yorker."

After the guy in front of her got out of the car because the machine that dispensed tickets on the autostrada wasn't working and yelled at the guy sitting in the booth, she inched the car up and pressed the red button to get her ticket. She drove onto the highway called Firenze-Mare (Florence-Sea), a romantic name for a highway, she thought. Soon she fell into her usual highway trance—how do these drivers not get into serious accidents? She dreamed about her first affair. Highway trances, however, are short-lived in Italy. She slammed on the brakes behind a Vespa motor scooter with a Mamma and Papa riding at 30 miles per hour.

"God damn it. How the hell did they get on this highway?" After waiting for six cars, two diesel trucks, one van and another motor-cycle to fly by her, she passed the out-to-lunch motorcyclists. They are crazy not to wear helmets, she thought.

She passed Torre del Lago, Puccini's summer vacation spot. It's so nondescript: flat and caked with gray smog. She wondered if there was smog in the early twentieth century. Someone ought to do a sociological study of smog and its effect on art. Every music histori-an knows those fifteenth-century smoggy songs dedicated to the cult of the fumeurs or smokers. Perhaps people created smog through excessive cigarette smoke. Fiammetta believed that smog existed through the centuries, even if environmentalists back home talked primarily about car emissions and refineries. Smog is an important part of culture. It shapes the way we view our place on the earth and our relationship to nature. It even has a feminist sig-nificance. Man pollutes Mother Nature, Mother Nature perseveres. Is there anything more beautiful than a sunset in smog? Red is Fiammetta's favorite color, hence her name: Little Flame. A person's name materializes way before a person is born. In a teaching evalu-ation, one student called her "irrevocably and flamboyantly provocative." This was something Reno couldn't fix.

She approached the exit for the city of Lucca. Lucca is famous for its medieval walls and a church that houses the tomb of Ilaria del Carretto, a member of the fancy Guinigi family who owned most of everything in the city in the fourteenth and fifteenth centuries.

A medieval ancestor of this family was named Castruccio
Castracani and a statue of him riding a horse decorates one of the
piazzas. His name means little castrator, dog-castrator.

She daydreamed again about Valerie, her old girlfriend with
whom she had been to Italy the last time. They had dated for two
years, but like many of her past eight relationships, this one didn't
work out because there was something fundamentally wrong: in
fact Fiammetta had written a poem on the subject. Poetry soothed
her prickly nerves.

Ode to Women

some married
some alcoholic
some afraid of intimacy
some with distant boyfriends
some too skinny
some with overbearing mothers
some with hateful fathers
some work too hard
some liars
some bisexual
some in therapy
some not
some afraid of open spaces
some play with their hair
some do coke
all not for me now.

Jennifer took her mother out to lunch at the Metropolitan
Museum of Art that day. Mom lived on the Upper East Side, so it
wasn't out of her way. Nothing that concerned Jennifer was out of
her way. She wanted to be with her daughter as much as possible,

needed to monitor her every move, because she did not feel like confronting her own moves. Typical of mothers, Jennifer thought as she climbed the steps of the museum and smiled at the guard standing there looking bored. Jennifer had forgiven her mother for her mistakes last year. She spotted Mom standing next to the information counter, their usual meeting point. They generally did everything the same way.

"Hey Mom." Jennifer smiled.

"Hi," she stopped. "What have you done to your hair?"

"What do you mean?" Jennifer was used to this question.

"I'm not sure if I like the way you got it cut. Too boyish. I wish you'd grow it a little longer. You'd look so much better."

Jennifer shrugged her shoulders. She didn't have the energy to explain she'd just spent $100 on the cut.

"What's new?" Jennifer changed the subject. Hair is a no-win situation for most daughters.

"Nothing much. Been volunteering a lot at the hospital. Oh, I've just got to tell you. I was sitting in Doctor Lubner's office and you wouldn't believe who came in."

"Who?"

"Peppino Folle, the opera singer. He was there with his assistant. He looked awful. Fat, puffy. He was such a big baby, too."

They made their way to the restaurant and a tall African-American waitress sat them in the cozy table next to the dessert rack.

"How is Simon?" Mom's eyes lit up whenever she thought of her beloved son-in-law. Simon could do nothing wrong in her eyes, and for that Jennifer was infinitely thankful.

"They've put him on a new account in L.A. I'm not too thrilled about him traveling. I'll miss him so much when he goes away."

"You'll have to adjust your schedule a little. You know your father traveled a lot when your were a child."

"I guess so."

"How is your job?" Her Mom had a litany of thoughtful and probing questions.

"Fine. Mr. Davis is selling a Renaissance drawing to Japanese investors. Experts assert it's a real Michelangelo, though there's really no evidence. It's unsigned and unmentioned by Michelangelo, but it does look like another work of his. Davis wants me to go to Florence to speak directly to the Italian owners. Deliver a key document."

"That's wonderful, dear. Why didn't you tell me about this sooner?"

"I don't know. I don't like the idea of going over there without Simon. He'd love an Italian vacation. I could show him the city." Jennifer fondly remembered the six months she spent in Florence during her junior year at Wellesley.

"When do you go?"

"Next week. Probably Wednesday. I'll stay four days."

"I'm jealous." Mom said. She should write Hallmark cards, but lacks the right connections.

The waiter brought them the check, and Jennifer thanked Mom for lunch and told her she would see her when she got back. Lunch with Mom was always pleasurable, but at the same time stressful, because Jennifer still saw herself as the spitting image of her mother. Her mother was superficial and pushy and for some reason Jennifer believed she also manifested these qualities. She said goodbye, picked up her purse off the back of the chair, and walked out of the cafeteria. Checking her watch, she realized she still had twenty minutes, so she looked over the newly-installed photography exhibition dedicated to the first hundred years of the medium.

Fiammetta parked the car under the shade of an elm tree. The rectangular torri of Cennina rose above like the twin towers. She pulled out her briefcase from the front seat, locked the doors, straightened her panty hose, and marched up the hill. It was a cool day for the middle of June, and Fiammetta felt chilled. The steep dusty road that led to the town was lined with new Italian and imported cars, and she was happy to see that there was a good turnout for the lecture series on the history and culture of Cennina. Coming to an ancient brick tower, and peering into its decrepit window, she saw a wooden vat and a wooden screw-press that was used to squeeze grapes. On the other side of the road stood the ruins of three homes. Each was invaded by ivy and filled with the remains of roofs and upper floors. The doorways stood intact. Fiammetta could read the house numbers that had been carved into the brick. Hundreds of years of Tuscan sun and wind had polished the bricks, and Fiammetta reached out to feel their texture. A green fly buzzed around her, landed on her hand. She flinched and it flew off into the ruins.

Gianni Vespri, the owner of this medieval village, greeted her at the top of the hill.

"Benvenuta professoressa," he said before kissing her on both cheeks twice. He showed her the refreshments, and she declined the kind offer of a glass of cold white wine in favor of a Coke. This was blasphemy in Italy, but she didn't care because she was dying for a Coke.

Gianni led her around the red chrysanthemums, plants that decorate all of Italy's balconies, to an imposing edifice—the remains of the Cennina church. Three walls were left standing. Gianni had rebuilt the roof and added a fourth wall.

"It's been such a problem. So expensive. I can't get people to come up here." He was resigned to his fate of spending vast quantities of money on a childhood dream. Me too.

Inside, chairs were set up in rows and a black lectern faced the audience. A medieval culinary scholar was giving a talk on the types of wines produced in the Cennina region. He droned on in that usual academic way. Gianni led Fiammetta to a seat and handed her a program. She was scheduled to speak after the next guy, who would be talking about a medieval manuscript that mentioned Cennina.

Fiammetta pulled her notes from her briefcase and glanced at them one last time. She did not like to read directly from a script when she spoke in front of people, opting instead for a more off-the-cuff presentation. Audiences seemed to focus on her discussion more, and she did not feel as if she was reading a book report in front of her second-grade class. After all, she pondered, wasn't scholarly work just one big book report?

Gianni introduced her as the great "feminist" musicologist from Reno who had written several books on the medieval period and the status of women.

"Good afternoon. I've just arrived from New York, and I hope you will forgive my somewhat disheveled appearance and pale complexion. I am here today to talk about a topic that will probably make some of you nervous: women. Women in Cennina. Why does the topic automatically cause some of us to feel uncomfortable? Why should I focus only on women? Isn't this rather limiting?" She continued by talking about institutionalized misogyny, starting with the story of Adam and Eve and moving to St. Paul and so on. Fiammetta had the audience right where she wanted them—listening to her discussion of the way women participated in the musical life of a medieval city. Upper-class women received music lessons on the harp and vielle, soft feminine instruments suitable for indoor playing. Aristocratic women were expected to spend most of their lives inside their chambers. They were forbidden to stand next to an open window or door for fear they might be misconstrued as available to suitors. We know less about women of the lower classes in the medieval period; they have been written out of history. After she was done, the audience applauded enthusiastically. Nevertheless, Fiammetta felt she had bombed irrevocably. She was working on these irrational feelings with her shrink in Reno. That's another book.

Gianni returned to her side and thanked her for the splendid lecture. He directed the audience to the courtyard for a little wine tasting. He had ordered several Chiantis from the region, and was interested in knowing which of these wines people preferred. "Now it's time for fun."

Fiammetta was walking toward the church exit when a graduate student came up to her. "I wasn't too dull, was I?" Fiammetta was most afraid of boring her audience. There should be mandatory jail time for boring an audience.

INTERMEZZO 1

Play all the black notes on the piano with the damper pedal down for six minutes and five seconds. Listen to your dreams.

STORY 1

Fiammetta's uncle shaped her life in the most unexpected ways. Just listen to this story.

Uncle Riccardo's Driving Lesson

Hiking under the shadow of the Matterhorn felt right—even if I'd never climb it. Besides, my Uncle Riccardo was gracious to come all the way across the Alps to pick me up the day after the Virgin Mary's B-Day (August 15th). He was not a practicing religious person. Riccardo was a champion ski jumper. "Jumped over a house once," he told me in English.

He was waiting in the tidy Geneva Airport baggage claim area and said he needed to do a couple of errands before returning to

Italy. He hated Italy because it was full of cretins. Nothing ran on time. His mother wasn't Italian but German and this, he said, gave him the upper hand when it came to monetary concerns. He put all his money in Swiss banks. When we got to his white Alfa Romeo Junior (1966, a classic), he opened the door, then opened the hood and showed me his money in the little plastic pouch that usually holds water to spray the windshield. Bills of Italian flowery money. "See," he said, "I hid it from the border police." Retrieving his money and closing the hood gently, he thought I should drive because rich people have chauffeurs. "Driving is bad for my shoulders," he admitted. I threw my valise in the trunk and ripped the keys out of his hand.

"We have to go to the store," he said. "I need more rice." I was weary after a night of microwaved goodies and tiny-screened entertainment. We traversed Lake Geneva on a cement bridge that flanked the Baume Mercier building. "Follow the right side of the road until you get to the top of the hill and make a left." He wanted Uncle Ben's Converted Rice, which you can't find in Italy. There was only thick, gooey Arborio risotto in Italy. Then he directed me to the bank. "I'll make a deposit; sit tight. I'll be right back." He jumped out in his wool sweater and wool undershirt; he was five feet, ten inches in height with bright blue eyes and ear lobes stuck to the side of his neck. "Stuck earlobes are a sign of nobility," he told me. He said we were aristocrats, descended from the Zumstein family of the Walser tribe, a people from Liechtenstein who traversed the Alps in 1778. We had a mountain peak named after us called Punta Zumstein. It is 4,416 meters tall and has claimed a few lives over the years.

Aristocrats don't work: they revel in dolce far niente, sweetly doing nothing. He spent time in the orchard picking cherries and apples, occasionally throwing an apple at a tomcat and laughing when he hit it. He flushed a litter of my grandmother's kittens down the toilet every spring. I heard the mother cat howl when he took them from her. When he was ten he found a shotgun and aimed it at his father cradling his son Mario on his lap. Father told him to put it down immediately, held out his hand and said, "Stop aiming the gun at us you crazy boy." Then Riccardo pulled the trigger. Shot out all the windows of the sixteenth-century veranda. He fled into the garden, where he spent the night weeping.

My mother said he was always playing tricks on people. In the summers he and a friend snuck into the local hotel, stole all the patrons' shoes left in the hallway, and threw them in the river. Then they put the vegetable seller's cart on the roof of the bus so her goods ended up twenty kilometers down the valley. At nineteen he was drafted into the Alpini, the Italian Mountain squadron. He knew they wouldn't take him if he was too skinny, so he starved himself for thirteen days. The army did not take him, because he ended up in the hospital with encephalitis, where the priest read him his last rites. But he survived and had to go to the army anyway after six months. He sang all the Alpini songs, accompanying himself on mandolin, and wore a brown leather bulbous cap with a feather sticking out of it. After two years of working on the railroad directing trains when to stop and start, he went to the university in Milan. He enrolled in the Languages Department because he loved English. He slowly stopped going to class and holed himself up in his tidy apartment. His father fished him out and took him to the hospital, the sanitarium where he received electric shock treatments and was sent home after a few months. He regained his weight and kept himself busy by berating the neighbors for being cretins and by stockpiling the family collection of Caruso records. He found and sold them all.

He could never hold down a job, favoring philately, trading family stamps. He had a huge collection from the British Colonies. He also relished his newfound power as landlord, assigned to him by his father who had numerous holdings throughout the Aosta Valley in Northwest Italy. Shepherds lived in a small chalet in Valsavaranche, and Riccardo visited them once a month to gather the rent (about $300) and inspect the property, which he understood would be his once his father died. He dressed in a long wool undershirt and baggy wool pants, always, even in July.

I waited in the car and played with the buttons for the heat. Nothing. My feet were ice for some reason. I pulled out my pumpkin-emblazoned diary and my pen and started to write. "My trip went well. Had two beers on the plane. Riccardo in the bank. I cannot keep my eyes open. I need some sleep." A tear welled up in my eyes, and I slipped the diary away when I saw him. He directed me to the green-labeled Swiss highway #E62 and asked me what I thought of John McEnroe. "He was good at Wimbledon," Riccardo said. Riccardo went to Wimbledon to eat strawberries and cream and drink champagne by himself. Elegant people vacation in England, not Florence. Florence is dirty and full of stupid Italians. England was Anglo-Saxon, the highest breed. Once he yelled at my father that he was sorry that they didn't get all of his kind in the Holocaust. That was after he told my brother never to step foot inside grandma's house with an Asian woman again, and that was after he wrote my aunt that she was a whore. After he told my mother that she was a disgraceful bitch.

I came to an abrupt halt on the crosswalk for a red light. A Swiss woman glanced at our Italian license plate and sneered at us. Riccardo rolled down the window and blew her a fart. We laughed.

Ha, ha, ha—who does she think she is? The Swiss hate the Italians by nature. Just see the movie *Bread and Chocolate* with Nino Manfredi. On the highway to Lausanne, Riccardo told me to take the car as fast as it could possibly go. One hundred fifty kilometers an hour rose to 160 to 170 to 180 to 190—then he told me to move into the right lane and put the car in neutral to see how far we could roll and save some gas. We rolled a good two kilometers, slowing to 60 to 40 to 20, and he laughed again until we stopped dead on the side of the road.

In Lausanne, on Avenue C. F. Ramuz, I waited for him to see his urologist. He had Swiss doctors because the Italians were cretins and to top it off incompetent. The last time we were together, Riccardo took me to the base of the Aiguille Blanche (under the Mont Blanc), tied me to a rope, and ran up the gentle side of the rock to teach me rock climbing. (Was that before or after he took me skiing in the town of Pila wearing his 2,15 meter skis and his #45 boots?) "Remember you need at least three places of contact for your legs and hands and never put your knee on the rock. Use your fingers and pull yourself up," which I did for a good twenty feet until I slipped and fell and the rope slid under my arm, burning my skin. That's enough. Then he took me on a hike on all fours toward the Aiguille Noire, told me I was capable of climbing the Matterhorn, which we would do in a couple of years, brought me to the town of Courmayeur, and outfitted me with the best Italian hiking gear, called Grivel. He bought me an ice axe, harness, gaiters, and glacier glasses. He lent me his leather rucksack and a pretty new red jacket. He gave me a book called *Scrambles Amongst the Alps* by Edward Whymper, the first to reach the summit of the Matterhorn and return intact.

Riccardo's book was covered in brown paper and had an English inscription on it: 68 College Road, S.E. 21, Oxford, 1937. It told the story, with wispy ink illustrations of needlelike peaks, of the 1865 ascent of the Matterhorn by a party of eight, of which only a few returned, the others sliding four thousand feet to their deaths after their rope broke. Riccardo recounted the story to me at least three times that day. In the back of the book I found nine typed pages of an English essay on the subject of Cretinism in the Aosta Valley. It explained why there are so many cretins in the city of Aosta and read, "It is supposed that cretinism arose from the habitual drinking of snow and glacier water." Riccardo was not a cretin. He was born of aristocratic blood, and aristocrats had no compulsion to mix with cretins. Cretini! Che cretino, che cretina, che cretini. What cretins. All of them. I don't think I'll ever climb the Matterhorn. I wished I could. I wanted to.

He jumped into the car and said that we are not going through the Mont Blanc Tunnel, which punctures the Alps at Chamonix in France and Courmayeur in Italy. We are headed for the Grand Saint Bernard Pass, where Napoleon crossed the Alps. Also we will not go through the Tunnel du Grand St. Bernard of 5.9 kilometers, we will take the scenic drive over the Alps at the Col du Grand St. Bernard. He said that he will give me a driving lesson on the curvy, skinny, asphalt road that crossed the Alps. In Martigny, the town before the climb up the Val d'Entremont to Bourg-St-Pierre, we stopped for a glass of lemonade because it was good for the kidneys. Riccardo's kidneys were notoriously problematic, from weird treatments I think. He ate only boiled vegetables and plain rice. Once a year he asked my grandmother to make him gnocchi—he lived with grandmother after grandpa died and took care of her after she had a stroke. They lived in Aosta, the home of cretins, and he refused to shop at the lattaia, the milk and cheese store, because

the owner was an insatiable gossip. Sometimes, in the late afternoon, he walked to a street corner in front of the Roman arena and
directed traffic for a couple of hours. He made angular gestures,
lunging like a fencer and then standing at attention. Some people
crossed the street when they saw him coming. He shouted at cars
that passed too close to him and said, "only stupid people shop at
the open-air market. They are only good at taking your money. Is
that a new friend you have? What does she want, your money?"

We jetted by the glacial Lac des Toules and navigated around the
entrance to the tunnel. A sign read 11% grade elevation and I began
to salivate at the thought of the windy road ahead. Few people
drive it anymore, Riccardo told me. It used to be the site of a
famous car race in the 1950s. He said I needed to learn to take the
curves as fast as possible. As I was driving the Alfa around a left-
hand turn he told me to accelerate through the curve. During the
next one, he told me to stay to the right, until the tires trampled the
little pebbles where the mountain flowers meet the road.
"Downshift to a lower gear and accelerate across the curve, not
minding that you will cross the center line into oncoming traffic. At
the end of the curve, shift to a higher gear." I was tentative at first,
not used to the feeling of being completely in the opposite lane of
the road. The idea, he said, was to take as straight a line as possible
through the turn. He repeated his same philosophy about skiing.
"Why turn when you can go straight?"

I took several left-hand turns fast, then we tried some right-hand
ones. This meant, he explained, that I was to take the car as far over
to the left as possible prior to entering the turn and then cut it off as
far right at the end. I had to swing way over into the other lane. He
encouraged me to try it, to get farther over, not to be afraid to
careen off the road. Never mind the three hundred-meter drop and

simple little white and red metal poles that separated the car from the bottom of the valley. Going up was the easy part. The descent is much trickier. That was on the Italian side: they have guardrails there. The more we drove, the faster I went. He said I was doing a good job until we reached the back of a slower-moving vehicle. I slowed down to a crawl and took a deep breath.

"What are you doing?"

"What do you mean?"

"Pass him."

"When?"

"Now."

"I can't see around the bend."

"Get as close to his behind as possible, in your lowest gear, and wait."

So I did.

"You aren't close enough. Get on him." And he made a downward gesture with his hand straight.

"Won't he get mad?"

Riccardo didn't respond. "Go, go, go. Your chance to pass him is coming soon."

Then he told me to step on the gas and pass him during a twenty-meter straightaway that separated two harrowing hairpin curves. "Go, don't worry, just go."

So I passed the guy with a smile and some relief.

"You must be more decisive next time. Get right on him. Don't let opportunities pass you."

We were quickly reaching the top of our journey at 2,469 meters. At the Great Saint Bernard Pass we stopped to get some more lemonade, and I went to the bathroom with my diary. "Riccardo has so much faith in me," I wrote. "No seatbelts. I feel free and frightened."

After the lemonade, I told him I was too sleepy to drive another kilometer. He took the wheel. "Are you sure?" he asked one last time.

He flew down the mountain with the precision of a fighter pilot in combat. When he encountered a slow car, he made a gentle move to the left, hard acceleration, and a return to our own lane. Easy. The vast, sunny expanse of the Great Saint Bernard Valley lay before us, and I asked him about this and that peak. "Have you climbed that mountain over there?" I asked and pointed.

"The Mount Velan?"

"Is that what it is called?"

"In 1952, with my friends Arturo and Paolo Squinobal."

"Those names sound familiar," I told him. They were his partners in pranks. Riccardo had helped bail out my partners and me last summer after we spent the night throwing mud balls at the priest's house. Who knew that they would stick and dry on the white walls? We couldn't see. The next morning Riccardo woke me up to say that the priest had come to our house demanding that something be done. While I slept, Riccardo took a hose to his house and washed off all traces of the mud balls. He was proud of what I had done. "Wish I had thought of that one when I was young," he told my mother.

I told Riccardo about our pranks with pride, because he was the only one who could ever see the art in them. Once we snuck into the church steeple and rang the church bells for half an hour before the local sheriff called us into his office. The sheriff came to my mother to report our misdeeds. She said we were bad children. Riccardo smiled. I asked him about his new wife Telma. "How are you doing?" Riccardo had married Telma, my grandmother's nurse, last fall. She had a daughter from a previous marriage and suffered from bouts of depression. He had never married before the age of fifty-six, never could keep a girlfriend for more than three months. Mity, my mother's best friend, was the love of his life—all he ever did was call her a witch. Telma found a home for her daughter in grandma's huge apartment, and a man who would pay the bills. Sometimes Telma would not get up out of bed for three days in a row. Her daughter Ada, twelve, laughed with Riccardo and played chess with him—sometimes Chinese Checkers. We drove past the town of Etroubles in Italy, where he reminded me of the apricot orchard he owned. He said he wanted to build a grass tennis court on that property to rival the Wimbledon lawns. Later we stopped in Gressan for another lemonade.

POEM 1

Multnomah Falls

As yellow leaves drifted down a woman with camera in hand rushed over to tell her friend this was the skinniest waterfall she had ever seen. Her friend wearing a pale green tight T-shirt and matching orange shorts agreed. They exchanged smiles and moved up the path slowly at andante tempo. And behind them a family of kids, one bigger boy lifting his little brother off the ground by his neck. And then running away behind his father's sneakers, the other kid rubbing his neck slightly, but not protesting. Clearly he had been lifted up by his neck a lot. The uptight girl from the East Coast, hair frizzy with anxiety and overprotective parents, sneered at them. She needed to leave home desperately.

She turned to look at the bridge that spanned the base of the falls. It was built in the early part of the century to entertain Oregonians and their families who needed a reason to stay in the state besides the fact that there was no sales tax. And that the summers were really pleasant and there was little if any pollution. "Watch where you are going," she wanted to tell the six-year-old blond girl with an orange ring around her mouth after being stepped on. But this was Oregon, land of children and patience. And big fathers.

Her mother did not want to climb all the way to the top. She had a bad heart since 1983 and did not want to chance another attack of heart palpitations. So they sat on an orange wood bench under a cedar tree, next to a wastebasket that read, "Bottles Only." Further down the path there was another bin that read, "Paper Only." Mom said that the mountains looked like upstate New York and that the river was like the Hudson and that the air was like the Alps and that the people looked like they were happy.

ART 1

Posing Backwards in Rome

Roman woman swats child
on behind
in Campidoglio.
"When I tell you to do something,
you should do it."
A literal translation.

No Messages

Rome sucks, cheated me at the hotel, neurotic friend. Eat artichokes, tourists laugh, period strong, Roman Emperor crustacion, spezzico

Changed tampon at 10:51 A.M.
campidoglio.

Posing Backwards

this policy because of the recent bombing of the Uffizzi Gallery."

"Better safe than sorry," Jennifer said. "I have an appointment at the Uffizzi tomorrow to meet the curator of the Michelangelo prints. I'm told that they will take me on a brief tour of the bomb sight. A real tragedy, that family and everything."

"They were in the wrong place at the wrong time." The hotel manager said as she completed the tedious paperwork. "Here is your key. You are in room 10 on the fourth floor. The bellhop will take your bags. Just a minute." She called for Luigi on the intercom.

A skinny middle-aged man with a matching mustache picked up her bags and led her to the elevator. Italian elevators are not much bigger than coffins and the man squished Jennifer and her two bags into the tiny space. He pressed the white button marked 4 and smiled. Jennifer noticed his odor almost immediately, and unlike New York City cabdrivers, this guy smelled like underarms more distinctly than curry, garlic, or some other spice. He didn't speak English, but that did not stop him from trying to start a conversation with Jennifer, whose only concern was to get out.

With his free hand to his mouth he began to gesture and said, "Mangiare."

"No," she responded.

Then he put his hand next to his face and asked if she was tired: "Stanca?"

"What?" She didn't get it.

Thankfully the elevator came to a stop. He led her to her room, asked for the key and unlocked the door. Jennifer found some lire and handed them to the smiling man.

"Thank you, miss."

"Prego." Jennifer said and locked the door behind her. It would take some time getting used to Italian men, if ever.

Fiammetta returned to her hotel at ten. They booked her a room in the Grand Hotel De la Ville, a four-star affair near San Lorenzo. Looked decent, she thought, as the bellhop grabbed her bags. She especially liked the marble floor and fake flowers in the lobby.

"Keep the change," she told the bellhop after he deposited her bags on her bed.

"Grazie signora," he said.

"Prego." Get out, she thought. He wasn't bothering her particularly. Didn't ask any intrusive questions about where she was from or how long she was staying. She just needed to be alone to assess her afternoon's performance. "Another lecture, another dollar," she said to the mirror facing her bed. Fiammetta had been in the professor business for three years. A doctoral student from N.Y.U., and in Reno for her first job, she began to think that this professor thing was really a piece of cake. The petty politics, the infighting, and the publishing had lost their ability to scare her into a night without sleep. She no longer dreaded criticism. She no longer feared for her tenured life. She no longer stayed up two weeks straight before delivering a lecture. She didn't much care. She had feared her complacency and supposed it was like anything: most of the pressure you experience in life is placed there by yourself. The downside to this incredible realization is that you become content. It was beginning to be old hat. "Well, at least I'm in Florence," she mused, "I could be in South Orange, New Jersey, giving this paper."

She took off her clothes and headed for the shower. The water coming out of the showerhead smelled like a combination of rotten eggs and dirty women's underwear, and Fiammetta cursed the Florentines for not taking care of their environment. Must be that Reno living. The clean air was clearly going to her head. She put her head under the stream and sighed as the first wave of hot water penetrated her hair and touched her scalp. She took the soap and rubbed it under each underarm and between her legs and her toes. She got out of the steamy shower, put on a T-shirt with a Yankees logo and looked out the window to the San Lorenzo church. Florentine lovers strolled in the dim streets and motor scooters still buzzed around. She sat down at the desk, opened the drawer and pulled out a piece of hotel stationary. A pen lay next to her right hand and she began to write:

> If yesterday the sun
> had set earlier
> the tree would be
> greener today.
>
> If she had
> said she
> loved me today
> I would not
> have just
> broken my arm
> falling off my bicycle.

She sighed and felt her heart sink slightly after rereading it. Life seemed empty for her now, like watching the Giants win the Super Bowl at home—alone.

She had nothing planned for the morning. Perhaps a jaunt to the Uffizzi? She was anxious to see the damage the bomb had done. Five people were killed. Lucky more weren't injured. She put on a sweatshirt and jeans and sneakers, grabbed some lire and her keys and walked out. Forgoing the elevator, she walked the six flights of carpeted stairs to the main floor and asked the concierge for the café.

"Behind the door near the stairs."

"Grazie." She wanted some tea.

The café glistened in the lights that shined on cakes and croissants. Did you ever hear the joke about the croissants?

Jennifer had a busy day ahead: breakfast with Antonio the museum curator, lunch with the owner of the picture and dinner free with her own thoughts. She put on her snappiest Evan Piccone suit—it was red—and sensible shoes. A last dusting of make-up applied, she called down to the concierge to get a taxi.

"It will be here in two minutes, madam. Please come down. They don't like to wait."

"Be right there."

She piled her notes into her leather bag, checked the mirror one last time, picked up her keys and walked to the elevator. There she met someone else waiting. She was mumbling to herself.

"Damn, these silly Italian elevators," said the tall, secure-on-her-feet woman.

Jennifer nodded.

"They are narrow as coffins," she was still complaining.

"Yes."

"Don't they bother you? I think I'll walk," she said and went down the stairs.

She must be from New York, thought Jennifer. Not that the woman had an accent, just the attitude.

Jennifer rode to the bottom where a frantic concierge was making gestures to move.

"Presto, presto, signora. He hates to wait."

"I'm coming." What's the rush, she thought, until she heard a symphony of horns and saw the cabby give the three cars waiting behind him the two-fingered cornuto sign. Then he got out of the car and walked toward the impatient motorist just behind him.

They exchanged what Jennifer could only make out as unpleas-
antries about someone's mother. Jennifer finally caught the cabby's
eye. He gave the driver one final gesture and directed all his attention to his beautiful, blond fare.

"Buongiorno, signorina," he said in a luscious baritone. He
opened the door for her.

"Buongiorno," she replied. "Vivoli's please."

"Subito."

They talked about Florence's cool weather for this time of year.
Italian weather words have many English cognates like tempo,
caldo, and freddo, and for this reason she was able to understand
him somewhat. It didn't really matter anyway. He wasn't listening.

Vivoli's is located near the church of Santa Croce. Tucked away in
the maze of small streets near Dante's birth house, the café is home
to American tourists and Florentines in the know for the best gelato
in town. She paid the cabby the fare on the digital monitor and then
some. He thanked her with a broad smile and a wave.

Vincenzo de Sabata was seated at the table near the doorway.
Dressed in a black Armani suit, his hair full of curls, he jumped up
and opened the door for Jennifer as she peered through the window.

"Jennifer McCall?"

"Vincenzo de Sabata?"

"Of course. It's a pleasure to meet you." He led her to his table
and helped take off her jacket. Slinging it over the adjacent chair, he
gracefully pushed the seat in under her rear end and sat down
across from her.

"Gianni," he called for the waiter.

"What would you like, Jennifer? May I call you that? A coffee,
perhaps cappuccino. You must try one of their pastries. They bake

them on the premises." She had so much to decide.

"Cappuccino sounds fine." She got up to look at the cakes and croissants behind the bright glass window. "And a croissant." A safe choice, even for her.

"Have a good trip? How is the hotel? I hope it is quiet. That neighborhood can be so noisy, especially during the day. I suppose that doesn't matter since you are out."

"Yes."

"How is Art, Art Davis? You know I met him here twenty years ago when we were both art students. Had breakfast with him every morning. Nice fellow. Good to work for, I am sure.

"Yes."

"Terrible tragedy the Uffizzi."

After the waiter delivered their cappuccinos and croissants, they chatted briefly about life in New York City and the time he visited there eight years ago, and how he liked Greenwich Village more than Midtown. She was learning that conversations with Italian men, at least the men she had met so far, were like driving down a one-way street the wrong way. After you realize your blunder you sit over by the side of the road, wait nervously for what seems to be an eternity for all the oncoming traffic to pass, as drivers gesture frantically, signaling that you are going the wrong way, and then you make your U-turn. Nothing much else to do in that situation.

He paid the bill, put her jacket over her shoulders, opened the door for her, and marched her down the narrow street toward the Uffizzi Gallery. He did everything. He continued to chat about politics and whatever else he could think of as enormous orange diesel buses drove by and the sound of motorini absorbed his voice. Like musicians who play in the New York City subways, he kept on going no matter how loud it got, even if she was busy making sure she wasn't stepping in some dog poop (there is a lot of this on the sidewalks of Florence) and avoiding oncoming pedestrians in a rush to get somewhere.

They turned onto the Piazza della Signoria, which opened up before their eyes like a flower in time-lapse photography. Here medieval men had sold their wares and now artists peddle cheap portaits. The sun severed the tower at midpoint and reached the gray cobblestones, filling up the piazza with light.

"This is magnificent." She finally got in a word.

The Palazzo Vecchio rose above her head flanked by a Renaissance loggia with four gray arches. Under each stood a bronze replica of a statue. One in particular caught her attention: Donatello's David, the rendering of a young boy displaying the severed head of Goliath in his hand. She loved this particular piece, and was moved even though she knew very well this was not the original. The original was in the Bargello Museum just around the corner. Proud of her knowledge, she followed Vincenzo past a line of museum-goers and into the entrance of the Uffizzi.

"Buongiorno dottore," the polite guard said to Vincenzo.

"Buongiorno Furio," he answered.

"Jennifer, I will show you the damage done by the bomb. Is that OK with you? I think it is of major interest. We are working day and night to shore up the structure."

"Fine."

They walked up the wide staircase and into Vasari's windowed gallery. Eager tourists running after naughty children flooded the space, and like champion slalom skiers the two made their way without running into anything. They reached the end of the corridor, which was cordoned off to the public. Signs read: "Attenzione, Vietato il ingresso," accompanied by an awkward English translation—"Attention, no entrance"—followed by translations in six different languages, some with characters, some with letters. A handsome carabiniere stood smoking a cigarette. He obviously recognized Vincenzo.

"Salve dottore," he patted him on the back. Then he took a look at his blond companion and smiled. "E la signorina?"

"Jennifer, Jennifer McCall. This is Patrizio."

"Pleased to meet you."

He nodded and looked at Vincenzo as if she were an inside joke.

Jennifer figured she should probably be flattered by this subtle exchange between men, even though deep down it pissed her off that she was valued for her looks rather than her brains. This would change the minute she saw the Michelangelo drawing. She would show them a thing or two about American women.

They walked around the metal barricades and into the relative darkness of the corridor. An odor of medieval bricks permeated the air. Perhaps it was the smell of the mortar, but she was suddenly reminded of her mother's dank basement in Bayside, Queens. Not that it was particularly medieval, but it was damp nevertheless.

"Watch your step, Jennifer." He pointed to some metal beams that had been placed on the ground.

"Feels like a tomb."

They turned right onto another long corridor. She looked ahead to find a hole in the marble floor.

"That's where the adjacent tower fell onto the gallery. We have cleared the bricks. We need to repair the floor."

"Where are the paintings?"

"In the basement. They were taken there immediately after the tragedy. Some damage to the Pontormos, but otherwise nothing major. If they had placed the bomb a few meters to the left it would have caused the collapse of the entire structure."

"Where was the bomb?"

"In a parked car behind the gallery. They shouldn't allow cars to park in the center of town. It's a wonder this hasn't happened before. We have lost some of our innocence."

They stopped a few feet from the opening and looked around. Pale lights lit the walls and it was odd that there weren't any workers there. Must be on strike, thought Jennifer. He grabbed her hand and led her back towards the carabiniere.

"Let's go to my office," he instructed.

Simon went down to Soho to check out the galleries this steamy summer afternoon. He hadn't been downtown in months and thought it was about time he caught up with the latest trends. Walking up Houston Street he thought about how he missed Jennifer. They never had time to walk around the city anymore.

Two women with cropped bleached hair and black leather jackets holding hands walked by. They must be lovers, he surmised. Simon was a pretty cool character, even though he did go to Harvard. Italian tourists bumped into him by mistake and said "scuzee" a hybrid of "excuse me" and the Italian scusa. He also knew they were Italian by their shoes—they weren't wearing sneakers—and their pricey Italian slacks. He remembered Jennifer again in Italy as he walked into the building that was home to the Sonnabend Gallery.

They had an exhibit of Jeff Koons's work. Simon was not ready to call his stuff art, especially after he opened the gallery door to a wall-sized photograph of a sex act. He winced with embarrassment and walked through a maze of people to a room that contained two wooden terriers on a white platform. This is much better, he told himself, as trendy Germans buzzed about. He then walked closer to the pale yellow Venetian glass sculpture of a man and a woman for-nicating. This was not quite as repulsive as the picture. He won-dered whether Koons sculpted this himself. Probably not. Koons has a remarkable flair for kitsch, and what better place to find kitsch than in pornography? Here is the post-modern update of the nine-teenth century's *Naked Maja*. Only Koons is funnier.

Simon courageously returned to the rooms with the enormous members on the walls. Each picture showed Koons and his wife in a different sexual position, leaving nothing, absolutely nothing, up to the imagination. The photographs had the air of Kodachrome gone mad. They made Michelangelo's newly restored Sistine Chapel ceil-ing appear to lack in color. Jennifer would be absolutely horrified. Good thing she missed this. He walked twelve inches closer to one entitled *Love*. At this distance the surface appeared grainy and the design dissolved into points of color. Much like Seurat. Was Koons really thinking about Seurat? Was Koons contributing to the vener-ated tradition of Western art? Was he just out to make a buck? And didn't he, since each image went for about $100,000. Was he a pub-licity hound? A demi-god? Who would ever be so self-indulgent? He really had to have some balls. Did he ever.

Simon made his way back down the narrow stairs into the late summer sunlight. Streams of people walked by him to get into the gallery. Strolling down the street, he came upon a man playing some kind of old instrument. A tambourine jingled around his ankle as his left hand turned a crank on an instrument. With his right hand he pressed wooden keys. A sign next to his feet read, "Hurdy-gurdy." Simon stood mesmerized by the sound of the instrument. A drone clung to his ears as the musician played a dance tune in some kind of medieval mode. He waited for him to stop, put some change in the basket and picked up one of his business cards.

It read: "Prof. Martin Bayless, Medieval and Renaissance music for any occasion. Tel 212 784-8904. No party is too big."

"Great sound," Simon said.

"Want to try it?"

"No."

"Come on. It's not difficult." Like a woman taking her purse off, he slipped the instrument over his head and handed it to Simon.

"Put the straps around your shoulders so you don't drop it."

"Got it."

"Turn the crank and press the keys."

Simon made music for the first time in his life. He was not sure what he played, but there was no denying that it was music. He felt his feet tapping and his heart pumping. He had dreamed of being in a rock band, only he couldn't play anything. Soon the professor joined him with the tambourine and then started to play a wooden recorder. They were jamming on the streets of Soho. Families with children stopped to listen. Single lovelorn people took a minute out from their despair to listen. Others wanted to try. Simon went on for three minutes but in reality it must have been ten. Time moves differently when measured in music. He stopped turning the crank. The crowd clapped and placed more money in the basket.

"Thanks. You have been a good sport," said the professor.

"Thank you."

"What's your name?"

"Simon."

"Simon. Martin. Pleased to meet you. Interested in buying any of my music?" He pointed to the hurdy-gurdy case. Simon bent down and picked up a cassette. He didn't really want any, but he bought one anyway.

"How much?"

"Ten."

"Here." He pulled out a crumpled ten from his pocket.

"Where did you get the instrument?"

"My Dad. He was a high school music teacher in Queens. Played everything. He played these instruments around the house. A one-man band." He pointed to a chart of early instruments. "Interested in buying my book? It was published by the Hurdy-Gurdy Club of America, of which I am president. Tells you where to get the best instrument and how to play it. But you may not need that. You seem to be a natural."

"No thanks. Hey, listen, it was nice talking to you. Take care now."

"You too."

Simon walked south on West Broadway towards a pub he liked.

INTERMEZZO 2

To play the blues, depress the keys C, E-flat, F, F-sharp, G, B-flat, in any combination on the piano. Imagine.

STORY 2

During a break from her dissertation research, Fiammetta wrote a story imitating Boccaccio's *Decameron* (Day III, Story 1). She told her dissertation advisor that it was an homage.

Zucchini

Book group met every Wednesday night at the Villa Ceci in the Tuscan town of Settignano. Six women attended; their husbands, professors on sabbatical, studied the fruits of Italian Renaissance ingenuity at the German Institute in Florence. Their husbands flaunted degrees from the University of Chicago, Harvard, and the like, and were united by fancy fellowships that coddled their egos and pushed their careers to dizzying heights past tenure. Their

wives, three of whom were former graduate students, appreciated a
reprieve from exhausting jobs in the United States for a few months.

The women stipulated a few rules during a boring dinner party at
the German Institute. Their book selections will have something to
do with Italy—they were in Italy after all! They will eat marvelous
food and drink lots of wine. They will allow each person to have
her say. No interrupting. Days were quite lonely for these women
more accustomed to high-powered computer programming and
managerial jobs than empty September afternoons. The women
were around the same age, in their middle forties. Their children, if
they had some, were home with nannies.

The current book under scrutiny was Patricia Highsmith's *The
Talented Mr. Ripley*, though some had seen the movie. Barbara said
that the writing was "insightfully engaging," while she sipped her
glass of Chianti Antinori. She organized a potluck dinner each time:
tonight featured pasta al pesto, veal cutlets alla Milanese, sautéed
red and yellow peppers with anchovies and capers presented on
baby-blue ceramic plates. Barbara was married to Bill, who taught
at a small liberal arts college in Denver. She worked for a computer
software magazine, edited the entire thing. She was the best copy
editor in Denver, and said of Highsmith's writing, "She has a strong
eye for detail. Her descriptions of the Mediterranean are riveting."

Anna agreed by nodding with a piece of prosciutto in her mouth.
Anna came with Bob, the hotshot Michelangelo scholar from
Columbia University. She ran her own catering business in New
York City called Annabanana. This was her first extended break
from it in six years. She strolled back off the veranda to use the
bathroom because she'd drunk a lot of San Pellegrino water that
evening.

The veranda overlooked the northeast end of Florence, its glittering street lights made bluish by the Fiat haze. Fig and walnut trees framed their view, purple hyacinths scented the air. Terracotta tiles polished to perfection lay at their feet, each worn a little more in the middle from centuries of pedestrian traffic. The food was presented on a white table-clothed oak table. Barbara scooped up a few more peppers and sat back down with the group.

"Highsmith certainly has the mind of a scientist," Barbara reasoned. "She almost dissects Ripley's comrades's faces."

It was Marnie's turn to talk. And she did, thought Barbara. Marnie fled her job as an Amherst, Massachusetts, urban planning bureaucrat. They'd granted her a short sabbatical to recharge her batteries. Marnie talked a little too much about how Highsmith's writing was full of irony, ironically. She cut off Barbara when she tried to interject a short aside about the last time she visited Naples. Then they agreed that Matt Damon was miscast. But he sure looked good in that skimpy bathing suit.

The doorbell rang. Barbara, the Villa's occupant, sprung up and said that it was Vanda, the young woman the Villa Ceci's caretaker Maria had introduced her to. "I've hired Vanda to be my private trainer. She's darling." Barbara skipped to open the door.

Vanda entered. She wore a black muscle shirt and tight gray shorts. Her shiny, mahogany hair was cropped short to her ears. Her skin looked as soft as that of a Raphael Madonna. As she walked into the room, her quadricep muscles rippled like a velvet tunic. She was about 5' 7" and waved confidently to the women of Settignano. She was Italy's second-best giant slalom skier in 1989. A mysterious bulge filled out her shorts at her groin.

"Vanda came by to give me a quick lesson on 'abs,'" Barbara chuckled. "Only night this week she could do it. Is that OK with you gals?" The women were glued to Vanda's unusually powerful look. Vanda greeted the crowd and found herself an empty portion of the red Persian carpet. She held out her hands and flashed her fingers five times. Then she proceeded to do fifty sit-ups. "Isn't she something," Barbara said delightedly, "and she speaks a little English."

Vanda had grown up in Florence and began skiing seriously at Abetone, a resort between Bologna and Florence. Her father, who owned a grocery store in the Santa Croce neighborhood, recognized her young talent and encouraged her with lessons and trips to races. Summers were spent training in Pila, a mountain village above the city of Aosta. The eighties were a time when Italian girls were given their first taste of the feminist movement. A convent was not the only option for a woman who did not want to marry. When Vanda's mamma's friends asked her why her daughter didn't marry, she said, "She is working on her career." But Vanda was working on her body and her look and other girls. She loved fast cars and women, and one could find her checking out the local beauties at the "Miss Arno" or "Miss Settignano" pageant. Vanda watched the contestants with a glass of wine in her hand and discussed the relative merits of their figures with a male friend. She fancied herself Mozart's androgynous Cherubino. "He is a farfallone amoroso (an amorous butterfly), " she explained to her friend. "I am an orsa amorosa (an amorous bear)."

Vanda first noticed the allure of women's breasts when she was thirteen. One day, while clothes shopping with her mother in the Piazza Della Repubblica, she literally could not keep her eyes off them. Each curve brought immeasurable pleasure to her groin. Her mother told her to stop walking like a boy, while she looked at her daughter's reflection in the store windows. "You move your thighs like a boy," Mamma said. "Too much like a boy," she shook her head in distress while in a store. "Here, try on this dress." No matter how many dresses her mother made her try on, nothing could stop Vanda from noticing girls. Nothing. Not even her mother's threat of estrogen injections. Those never materialized, luckily.

Vanda drove an old sporty Alfa Romeo Junior and made some money on the professional ski circuit. She'd recently gotten a job as a gym instructor on the Via Tornabuoni in Florence. The gym featured treadmills, stationary bicycles, and a shiny cappuccino and biscotti bar. Vanda was seen about town with tanned, big-haired housewives out of Fellini's 8 1/2, lonely for company and a good time. Her Santo Spirito neighbors followed her exploits but never said anything. She was a local star and deserved local star treatment, which in Italy meant privacy and turning the other cheek. But lately, she realized that she needed to be a bit more discreet around her new job (even though, as she explained to Maria, her childhood friend, and caretaker of the Villa Ceci for the last fifteen years, married women came on to her all the time). Maria told her about the women's book group in Settignano. She thought that the women might be interested in getting some physical exercise too. This idea was part of Maria's plan to win Vanda's affection.

Maria had been in love with Vanda since puberty and spent their summers together running around the hills of Abetone and sleeping on top of each other during outings in rustic hiking cabins. Maria wanted Vanda all to herself but understood Vanda's needs to sow her zucchini. In the meantime, Maria had found a great job through her family's connection to the Villa Ceci. She did light housework, shopped, and did laundry for the occupants, all of whom were connected to the German Institute.

Finished working her abs, Vanda began moving on to some push-ups. At this point she motioned to Barbara to follow her. "No, No,"

Barbara said, giving her the internationally understood stop sign. "Later," she pulled Vanda aside and into the kitchen, where they embraced and Vanda kissed Barbara gently while pushing her thigh into her groin. "Oh, my dear, not tonight. Domani, domani." Reaching for Vanda's crotch, Barbara said, "Domani," and, "don't forget your zucchini."

"Si, si. Signora."

Vanda and Barbara returned to the curious women. Marnie also seemed interested in some exercise. On a piece of paper she wrote down her telephone number and her name and slipped it into Vanda's hand. With one last Tuscan smile, Vanda said, "Buona sera," and left in her hot car.

The women returned to discussing the intricacies of Highsmith's plot, the double-entendres, and use of sprezzatura. All were feeling heated by the evening's events, liberated in the knowledge that none of the others could possibly be feeling what they were feeling.

The next week, while discussing the merits of Umberto Eco's *The Name of the Rose*, Marnie confided in Sarah, another wife.

"I've been getting private training from Vanda," she snickered, "and her zucchini." She broadened her smile and continued. "Are you interested?"

Sarah didn't hesitate. "At your house?"

"No. We meet in a private room in the back of the gym she works in. It's the massage room." Sarah nodded with enthusiasm.

"Slip her your number. She knows what to do with it." Marnie then picked up a piece of bread and sprinkled some olive oil on it. Returning to the group, Marnie said, "Eco's style is particularly engaging, his prose lucid, his wit clairvoyant." Meanwhile Marnie was thinking about her last session with Vanda. Vanda taught her the intricacies of a strenuous workout with the zucchini and the advantages of leather straps and a harness. "Grazie, grazie," Marnie had moaned.

"How was your workout yesterday?" Sarah asked Marnie, anxious to find out more during the next brief timeout from Eco's medieval monastery.

"Fabulous. My butt muscles are getting tighter and tighter."

"I'm sure." Sarah smiled. The doorbell rang.

"Vanda, come in," Barbara motioned. "You all remember Vanda."

The women nodded. Vanda was wearing very little tonight and her muscles were bronzed and tight. Her breasts, of tiny proportion, stood at attention. She was carrying a small black gym bag.

"I've asked Vanda to come by and give me a hand with some wood I need to move from outside into the garage." Barbara made an attempt at hand signals indicating that she needed wood picked up. "Won't you please excuse us for a few minutes."

"But of course," the women agreed and they returned to chatting about medieval logic and treachery. Eco's style sure was great, they thought. "He is a scholar at heart. You can tell he knows his Saint Augustine's Confessions," Sarah said aggressively.

Barbara returned, her face aglow from the zucchini, and escorted Vanda to the door. "This was the only night Vanda could help me out," Barbara explained to the group.

Sarah got up and walked over to Vanda, tapping her watch and holding a piece of paper with her telephone number in her hand. "Domani," she whispered.

"Si, signora," Vanda responded. Judy and Iris, former graduate students in French music, leapt up off their chairs and tucked their telephone numbers in Vanda's cut-offs. They both made motions lifting imaginary weights. Vanda nodded, and Judy and Iris agreed that they needed to work on some trouble spots themselves. Judy pointed to her back and said, "I need special attention because I sit all day in front of a computer." Vanda seemed to understand. Iris felt the same way. After Vanda departed, Barbara, Marnie, Sarah, Judy, Iris, and Anna sat back down and ate bruschettas and mozzarella and tomatoes. The sun drifted into the shores of the green Arno as Sarah communicated her absolute horror over the plot's denouement.

During the next two weeks, the six women enjoyed Natalia Ginzburg's autobiographical *All Our Yesterdays*, and Giorgio Bassani's gripping *The Garden of the Finzi-Continis*. Marnie discussed the merits of a strong plot line, while Judy noted the advantages of satire. Each woman's muscle tone gradually became more defined. During the breaks for more wine and food, Sarah flaunted her newly found triceps muscles. Barbara lifted her shirt and pointed to the six quadrants emerging from her abs. Marnie had recently located her lateral muscles. "I can do three sets of ten with five-kilo weights," she said as she motioned her hands up and down in a rising fashion. Each was particularly pleased with Vanda's services. The husbands, unsuspecting of their wives' adventures, approved of their sculpted bodies and new zest for life. "Larry really likes them," Marnie said about her "lats."

The next day, a weary Vanda knocked on the back door of the Villa Ceci to speak to Maria. "I can't go on like this. I am exhausted."

"Come in," Maria motioned, and sat her friend down near a huge oak table that flanked a black fireplace. "Want some coffee?"

"Yes." Vanda told Maria about her rigorous schedule. "I see Judy on Monday, Barbara on Wednesday, and Marnie on Friday; Sarah on Tuesday, Anna on Thursday, and Iris on Saturday. It is too much for my zucchini." She continued to talk about the relative merits of each client: the extra tips she received from Barbara, the flowers from Marnie, the jewelry from Sarah, the silk scarf from Judy. "And my back is starting to hurt."

Maria set a fuming espresso before Vanda. "It is too much," she agreed. "They want too much from you."

Vanda swallowed the coffee like a shot of vodka and asked her friend what she should do. Maria, a person of great integrity and ingenuity, came up with a solution. Over a few homemade biscotti and a glass of chilled white wine, Vanda listened and nodded. She looked down at her watch and bounced up off the chair. "I have to go back to work. Sarah is waiting for me."

A month passed. The women became healthier and healthier. They cut out salami and cheese (alas, no more pecorino). They began jogging together in the rugged hills above Settignano. They met every other morning at 10:00 and discovered trails around prickly blackberry bushes and olive trees. One day they stumbled upon a mysterious grotto carved into the rusty earth. Inside the air was damp and cool. Postcards of the Madonna were tucked into the rocks. The women experienced the peaceful surroundings and emptied their minds of fears. They chatted about the length of the line at the Uffizzi Gallery and their husbands' lecture preparations. Bemoaning the fact that there were only three weeks left to their stay, they agreed to stay in touch after they returned to their respective careers and lives—no matter what.

Wednesday night they met at the Villa Ceci to discuss Anna Magnani's biography. "I loved her in Rome, Open City and Bellissima," Marnie said as a tear welled up in her eye. "And to die so tragically of cancer." The women were wearing their emotions on their sleeves. At the break they ate tofu and anchovy salad. A bright-red tomato salad with red onions and extra virgin olive oil followed, which they sopped up with some Tuscan black bread.

The doorbell rang and Maria got up quickly to open it from her station in the kitchen.

Well-oiled and tanned, but droopy-eyed, Vanda entered the door carrying a big cardboard box. She held it in front of her chest, which served to highlight the definition of her biceps and triceps. The women looked at their trainer with pride. Vanda put the box down on the carpet.

She said in English, "Hello signoras. How are you tonight?"

The women looked at each other and all smiled. They had all experienced the pleasures of Vanda's exercise program.

"To be honest with you," she said walking over to the group seated in the living room, "I am tired. I have too many geese to feed."

The women nodded sympathetically. Sarah said slowly, "Vanda. I am sorry. I perhaps took advantage of your good nature and expertise."

Judy and Marnie concurred. Vanda opened her box and began talking about the benefits of good exercise. She handed each woman a workout schedule she had designed. Then she said that each could purchase a zucchini from her for 300,000 lire or about $150. Vanda explained that while these models were probably more expensive than those they could find back home, these had the advantage of Italian design and comfort. There was also no such store from which to purchase them in Florence. They jumped at the chance. Barbara found her pocketbook and reached for some money. She pulled out an object in a black-velvet cover from Vanda's box. Undoing the string to give it a quick inspection, she was satisfied and completed the transaction. Each woman followed. Some wrote her a check. Maria watched the proceedings with delight. Her plan had worked. The women were satisfied with their purchases. Vanda had learned a lesson: it is better to feed one goose with one zucchini than a whole gaggle.

Vanda stopped servicing women for good and took a brief holiday in Sardinia to recover from all the stress. Upon her return to Florence she moved in with Maria, who had decided to leave the confines of the Villa Ceci and start her own business. Vanda felt greatly indebted to Maria for her goodness and generosity of spirit and vowed to remain true to her. Maria confided her love for Vanda and nursed her back to full strength so that they could open their own book and zucchini store for women and begin a life together. The book-club women showed their gratitude by giving Vanda and Maria some extra money to start their business. Their store flourished and they made enough money to buy a little apartment in Fiesole.

The women of Settignano continued their weekly book meetings, ran together, and enjoyed Vanda's toys. Some introduced their zucchini to their curious husbands, who for the first time in weeks stopped worrying about their status and exercised their own. The women learned that their brainiac jobs were not enough to make them happy. They needed better physical stimulation. Back home they cut down their time at the office and spent more time with their families. Their husbands followed suit, forgoing meetings with needy graduate students for Tuscan dinners at home. The women began their book club over the Internet, downloading their favorite titles and posting their reviews. Once a year they met at Barbara's home in Denver and reminisced about the hills of Settignano.

POEM 2

Family Portrait

They reserved
four distant seats:
14E, 10B, 36B, 26F.

The son, in smoking,
impressing the tanked-top
woman with his smile.

Mom, close to the captain:
"I want to make sure that
he no make no mistakes."

Skittish sister writing in her
pumpkin-emblazoned diary,
covering the lines so 14D will not read.

Dad, well Dad
Sleeps, snores and complains that
the movie was pitiful.

ART 2

Doggy Yoga

Fiammetta picked up *La Nazione* and put it back down again. Satisfied with the previous day's performance, she no longer felt like doing anything intellectual. She looked out the window and decided to call the local gay group. Maybe there would be something fun to do tonight. Maybe she could meet someone. She had never known an "out " Italian lesbian. This was her next research project.

She found the phone book in the first drawer of the night table and looked for "gay," the international term for homosexual. And sure enough, even in repressed Italy, as in most repressed towns in the United States, there was a local gay hotline. She dialed downstairs to get an outside line and punched the six-digit phone number. "Phone numbers in Italy are so weird," she thought. Some have seven digits, some five, some six. Area codes are also of different lengths. They must reflect the Italian irregularity, and she was not only talking intestinal—she laughed to herself—or maybe the comfort they find in confusion, chaos. She heard the phone ringing.

"Pronto," a female tenor answered.

"Yes. Do you speak English, please?"

"Yes, a little."

"Good. I am a lesbian and would like to go out tonight. Do you know of any clubs or parties?" She said slowly.

"There's a gathering tonight at the Club Wings. A lecture about lesbian life in Florence."

"Great. Give me all the details."

"It's titled 'Mamma's Daughters: Lesbians in Florence.' It is in Italian."

"That's fine. What is the address?"

"Via Alfieri 57 red. At 6:00 P.M. No charge."

"Where is Via Alfieri?"

"Three blocks behind the Duomo toward Santissima Annunziata, you know the museum with Michelangelo's David."

"Of course. I am planning to see it this afternoon. This will work out fine."

"Anything else?"

"Will you be there tonight?"

"Probably."

"My name is Fiammetta."

"Francesca." So musical!

"I look forward to meeting you." She was constantly laying groundwork.

"Yes."

Satisfied with her attempt to meet some Italian lesbians, she plopped back on the bed and flipped on the tube. The Italian home shopping network came on. A large woman dressed in bright red was screaming into the camera at the top of her lungs.

"What are you waiting for? Why let those miserable hours, days, weeks pass? Get up. Get out. Get Vitamangia. With Vitamangia you will lose six kilos in one week—and eat good food. Eat pasta—no sauce. Eat lasagna—no butter. Just eat. But you don't have to eat rabbit food. You eat good Italian food. Food your mother, your grandmother made you." She gasps for air, like Fiammetta's Aunt Magda after a day of smoking True Blues. "Don't wait, don't hesitate. You get all this, the vitamins, the cookbook, the video, the Vitamangia hat, all for 100,000 lire. Wait. This week is special." She moves into sotto voce. "For you, my dear customers, this week the first fifty callers will receive this lifesaving remedy for just 69,000 lire. 69,000. Did you hear me?" The woman goes back to screaming mode. "Did you hear me? 69,000. Call, call. Now."

Fiammetta turned it off. She couldn't take all that shouting. Anyway what a dumb thing to be doing in Florence. Watching TV. She felt slightly embarrassed by her impulse to flip it on and decided to get an early start on the museums. Maybe she would start with the Uffizzi. Yes the Uffizzi, sounds good.

Vincenzo led Jennifer into his office. His door dated from the fifteenth century. "Look," he said. "See the termite holes in it and a relief of a Madonna and child at eye level." His office must have been some kind of place to pray. He turned on the lights. There were no windows, only vaulted ceilings above tall walls and a terra cotta pavement.

"You like?"

She nodded yes.

"The Medici family used this room. See that door over there?" He pointed and she looked.

"That door leads out onto the corridor that runs along the Arno

River and across the Ponte Vecchio to the Pitti Palace."

"I see."

"I will take you on a tour later." Jennifer suddenly realized that this would be a very long day.

"Please sit, sit down." He pointed to a green velvet couch in front of which was a flat coffee table. "Do you have the envelope?"

"Yes." She pulled out a tightly wrapped brown parcel and gave it to him.

"I'll get the drawing."

Behind a thick curtain, he started tinkering with the combinations of a safe. A final click and it was open.

"It is magnificent, no?"

She could not really see it from such a distance.

"Bring it closer, please."

He laid it carefully on the table. Mounted in an elegant, simple wooden frame, the drawing itself was about eighteen inches by eighteen inches, and done in reddish pencil. It was a representation of a twisted male nude with his back to the viewer. Massive arm muscles protruded from the paper and the subject's expression was forlorn and curiously empty. It looked a bit like the sculpture in the Medici Tombs of San Lorenzo. The torso, twisted especially in the upper back, followed the contour of the page.

"Yes, it is quite beautiful," Jennifer said finally after a well-defined inhale.

"It's the greatest discovery we have made in the last ten years. A Michelangelo drawing."

"Yes." She paused and then her true inquisitiveness emerged.

"Where are its documents?" She finally mustered the courage to ask.

"Documents?"

"Proof that it is by the great Florentine master."

"No such thing Signora Jennifer." His voice was suddenly more intense. "It is a sketch, a drawing, no need for proof."

"How can you say for sure that it is not a copy?"

"Well, can't you see, Jennifer, that it is a sketch of the Medici tombs? Who else would have made it? Please stop fooling around. We are talking a lot of money here. Please. Please. Uffa."

He was degenerating into baby talk. "Your boss, he already saw it. He knows it's authentic. There is no need to question that. He just wanted you to make sure it was in good condition. No need to doubt its value. One million dollars. We settled on it, Signora Jennifer."

Jennifer could not help but feel there was something fishy. Where did the drawing come from? Who had it before Vincenzo? Why did it just suddenly appear out of nowhere? Where was the proof? But this was obviously not the time or the place to debate the authenticity. Jennifer felt slightly used. Her boss did not want her to value the picture. That had already been done. He just wanted her to deliver the package. Any imbecile could have done that. But her instincts told her that the drawing was a fake, like the many done during Michelangelo's time. Students made copies to learn technique and contemporaries imitated the sculptures, hoping some of the genius would rub off on them. Jennifer had done this in her own studio painting class. Before beginning to work on their first canvas, her professor asked students to make a pencil drawing of their subject. Many rushed-off into the library to dig up their favorite image, Mona Lisa's expression, Michelangelo's David, Ingres's nudes. It was elementary. She needed more proof.

"Vincenzo, is it possible for you to take the picture out of the frame? I would like to look at the paper."

"Sorry. I cannot do that. It might get damaged." He was right. What was she thinking? "Mr. Davis has done this already. So have all the experts. That reminds me. I have those documents. Six art historians swear that the drawing is authentic." He got up off the couch, went to the file cabinet and pulled out a file.

"Here, take this. I made you copies."

"Thank you."

"Do you have a picture of it? I'd like a copy for my files."

"You don't have one already?"

"No. Mr. Davis did not give me one."

"Well, sure." Vincenzo became progressively upset. He was not prepared for Jennifer's inquisitive nature. He thought this would be a show and tell.

He walked over to his desk, pulled open the drawer and fumbled for a photograph.

"Here." He flipped the photograph onto the table.

"Thank you. Are you sure that there are no documents? No payments, no records of Michelangelo making sketches for the tomb?"

"No, no. That is not how it was done. Please, Signora Jennifer. You American art historians have come over here for centuries to tell us about our own painting. Would you like me to come to America and explain to you about apple pie and Andy Warhol's soup cans? We have been very patient with you. We understand Michelangelo. He is ours, no matter how you try and take him." He was starting to sweat slightly at the brow.

"I suppose."

"Jennifer, I am sorry to have to cut our time short, but it seems I have forgotten about a business meeting this afternoon. I have not prepared a word of my presentation to the board."

"I understand." She felt relieved.

He got up and showed her to the door.

"Will I see you again?" he asked.

"Is there a reason to?"

"I suppose not. You declare that the piece is in good shape?"

"Yes."

"When do you go back to New York?"

"Tomorrow afternoon."

"Perhaps we can meet each other for coffee tomorrow morning."

"Yes. That would be fine."

"Good, good Jennifer. The exit is down this corridor to the left. See. Then make a right down the stairs."

"Thank you."

"A domani," he said and shut the beautiful door behind him.

She waited for a second and then for a few more. She put her ear to the Madonna and child and heard him speaking in a loud voice. "Art. What in the hell." The guard walked by, looked at her legs and said, "Buongiorno signorina."

Caught snooping, she smiled the prettiest smile she could muster and walked down the hall.

Fiammetta walked down the narrow streets in combat mode. She was elbowed by three German tourists, yelled at by some punk on a motorcycle, practically run over by a diesel bus, and bombarded by pigeon droppings near the Baptistery.

"Ugh," she said wiping white stuff off her arm with a tissue. "This is disgusting." Then she thought better of the situation and made a wish. Bird poop wishes have a higher frequency of coming true. More so than wishbones, 11:11 on your digital clock, nuns on the street, brand new socks, or Chinese paper. Bird poop is the best. Waiting for the light to turn green, she wished to find the woman of her dreams. To finally settle down, start a family, and share a life with someone. Though she wasn't particularly dissatisfied with her life of many affairs, torrid evenings, and furtive looks at women, she began to think it was about time she settled down. At least she was beginning to feel the pressure from her family, especially from her mother who said that because she was a lesbian she would never have the stability of marriage. "What will you do with no one to care for you when you get old?" It was time to prove Mamma wrong.

She walked up to the museum and stood in line behind a French family with three dogs. An enormous handwritten sign read, "No Food, No Flash, No Pets, No Guns, No Drinks, No Grenades"—no it didn't—"No Bags." Satisfied that she didn't have any of those items, Fiammetta paid the fifteen thousand lire (isn't that outrageous) and was given the cheapest, flimsiest ticket ever issued (not like in Greece where the ticket at Delphi had a reproduction of the ruin I was visiting). A pretty Florentine then took half of it from her and stamped her hand with a green "D." She couldn't imagine some European member of the Green Party liking this idea. Didn't the ink seep into her veins and give her a small amount of poisoning? No matter. Fiammetta looked at it with admiration. This was like the stamp you get walking into any gay bar in New York. Now she was stamped "D." How very appropriate. She walked passed a table filled with slides, postcards, books, and posters. "I'll do this on my way out." Fiammetta liked conversations with herself.

Simon pulled up his socks and searched for the right jacket. Over two hundred and fifty suits were in his closet. He scavenged local Salvation Army stores every weekend for over twelve years and bought only Armani, Valentino or Ralph Lauren suits. He paid fifty dollars for clothes worth over seven hundred. He was compulsive about it. Dragged Jennifer with him sometimes. Or an unsuspecting friend.

His heart raced when he came upon one in the Ave U store in Brooklyn last week. He didn't even have to look at the label. This was obviously Armani, he thought to himself with pride. The sleeves and legs were a little too long, but his tailor, Mr. Wong on Broadway, could perform miracles. He didn't even mind that smell like the inside of rented bowling shoes (something that made Jennifer sick to her stomach). He put the suit under his arm and continued to rifle through for anything else of interest. Perhaps a nice silk tie to match, or a shirt with an elegant French collar. He noticed a man he had seen before enter the store and he began to sort through the clothes at a quicker tempo. That guy was here for the same reason. That guy was his competition. Got him this time. Sucker. Satisfied that he had found the suit, Simon walked over the register and paid the twenty-five dollars.

He chose a double-breasted brown linen Valentino for this afternoon's business meeting. It was perfect for those stuffed upper management stiffs who were slowly dying in their jobs and reading *Penthouse* during their lunch hours with the doors locked. They were a pitiful lot. Dave the divorcee, whose great claim to fame was his season tickets to the Giants games, and Bill, who had three kids, the perfect wife, and slept with his secretary Brenda on business trips. The hypocrisy of it all really bothered Simon. He wanted more. But how? How were things to change? They needed to pay back their loans that amounted now to $70,000, or was it $65,000? He couldn't just quit. It would take at least four years to pay for that. This left him with no options. Nothing. He walked into the living room and turned on the CD player, popped in Natalie Merchant's latest. God, what a great voice. He heated up a pot of coffee and put some bread in the toaster. He liked apricot jelly, no butter, on his toast every morning. Perhaps he would go to the gym this afternoon. That would make him feel better. He prepared his gym bag with a T-shirt, shorts and sneakers. Finished with his coffee, he walked out of the apartment and rang for the elevator.

Jennifer did not take another breath until she reached direct sunlight. She bent her head over her chest like a basketball player refueling on oxygen at the foul line. She quickly glanced around to make sure that Vincenzo wasn't following her and decided to rush back to her hotel then get the hell back home. Why, these lousy sons-of-a-bitches. Did they think she would be so incompetent, not to notice their ruse? They were peddling a fake Michelangelo. A decent fake, but still a fake.

She walked in a daze down the Via Tornabuoni and into the Piazza della Repubblica. She could have been in Queens for all she was aware of her surroundings. Eyes fixed on the ground, she planned her next move. Get home to New York and quit her job. What else could she do? Call the police? Call the philanthropist who was about to drop $1,000,000 on a poor copy? Simon. She needed to speak to Simon immediately.

She found a payphone in the alcove of a pizzeria. After waiting for some guy smoking a cigarette to finish cooing to his mistress, she grabbed the phone, punched in twenty or so phone card numbers and Simon's work number, and waited for the ringing to begin. One, two, three. She was starting to sweat through the armpits of her tasteful suit. Come on. Come on. His secretary Fiona picked up.

"Simon McCall's office," the Brooklyn voice announced.

"Fiona."

"Hey Jennifer. So how's your trip going?"

"Fine, fine, I'm sorry it's kind of an emergency. Is he around?"

"He just left for a meeting downtown."

"Damn. Tell him to call the hotel tonight."

"Anything else?"

"No. Don't worry him too much. I'm fine. Just need some advice. I'll be home tomorrow night anyway."

"Anything I can do, Jennifer?"

"No, Fiona, thanks. Just give him the message."

"OK. Take care, dear."

She hung up the phone and looked around. No sign of Vincenzo. Or that creepy guard. She swung her purse around her shoulder and walked down the street. That's when she recognized someone she knew. It was that woman in the hotel this morning. She was mumbling something to herself. Looked frustrated. Jennifer crossed the street and ran up to meet her.

"Excuse me."

"Yes," Fiammetta turned around.

They stopped to look at each other carefully.

"You are staying in my hotel, aren't you? I saw you this morning waiting for the elevator." Jennifer mumbled.

"Yes, of course. Sorry. I am so out of it. This creepy guy just tried to hold my hand while I was walking down the street." Fiammetta looked at her intently and being a native New Yorker was not afraid to ask her a personal question right off the bat.

"Did you get mugged or something?"

"Not exactly."

"Did you pay too much for something? No. Are you lost?"

"It's nothing like that. Do you have a minute? Can we have a coffee?"

"Sure. I'm on my way to a lecture." She checked her watch. "I have a half an hour. And knowing those Italians, it will probably start late."

They crossed the street to Gilli's and sat at a table near a minia-
ture palm tree. Jennifer introduced herself formally as married and
originally from Ohio. She told Fiammetta that she was in the art
business and lived on the Upper West Side. Fiammetta said she was
from New York City and had recently moved to Reno of all places,
making her first career move as Assistant Professor of Music at
Reno State. They had more in common than one would expect most
strangers to have on a chance meeting, and they talked about that
phenomenon briefly.

Fiammetta recognized Jennifer's fine features, lovely eyes and full
lips. Jennifer didn't really know what to make of Fiammetta, except
that she looked incredibly intelligent in a kind of George Sand way.
They liked each other immediately because they didn't trust anyone
else in Florence. Jennifer finally came to the problem.

"I've become unwittingly involved in a plot to sell a phony
Michelangelo drawing."

"Wow. How exciting."

"My boss sent me over here to make final arrangements for a deal
on a Michelangelo and after I saw the drawing this morning, I knew
it was a fake."

"How?"

"I can just tell. It was a copy. Probably by a contemporary of
Michelangelo's."

"I can tell a fake Haydn piano sonata if I hear one."

"I saw the drawing for the first time this afternoon. This cheesy
guy at the Uffizzi showed it to me in his office. I couldn't help but
reveal that I thought it was a phony. Thinking back I probably
shouldn't have."

"How did he react?"

"He was angry. I heard him on the phone with my boss after I left."

"What's the drawing worth?"

"Three thousand dollars if a copy, a million if it is real. What should I do? I don't know. I'm scared."

"Perhaps you should go to the police?"

"Do you think?"

"So they don't think you are part of the conspiracy."

"I have been trying to get a hold of Simon. He'd have some good advice. He always makes more sense than I do."

They talked more about options and drank decaf cappuccinos and had some salty olives. Jennifer calmed down a bit. She stopped sweating.

"When do you leave for New York?" Fiammetta asked.

"Tomorrow on the one-thirty flight out of Pisa for London and then connect to New York. How about you?"

"I've got a flight leaving from Milan on Thursday. I was planning to see some friends up there. Take the train tomorrow morning."

"Do you mind if I ask you a personal question?"

"Go ahead," Fiammetta braced for the one about her sexuality.

"What are you doing tonight? I mean."

"I'm attending a lecture." She remained vague.

"Would you mind it terribly if I came with you?"

"No," she hesitated slightly. "No."

"Good. Thanks so much."

"It's about lesbians in Florence."

"Oh, I see."

"I am gay."

"Oh, I see. So is my sister."

"Really." Fiammetta was relieved.

"Yes. She came out to my family when she was twenty. I knew it all along. She just wanted to play basketball. I found her crying in front of her best friend's picture one night."

"I'm glad to hear you are so enlightened. You just never know how some people will react to the news."

"I understand. Some people can be very cruel."

Fiammetta couldn't help but ask. "Have you ever been with a woman?"

"Yes." Fiammetta's heart filled with hope. "When I was in college I fell in love with a woman in my English class. We saw each other for about a year. I hid it from everyone." It was Fiammetta's turn to sweat.

"I'm sorry to cut this short," she looked down at her watch, "but the lecture begins in ten minutes and it will probably still take us fifteen minutes to get there." Fiammetta asked the waiter for the bill and paid for it in its entirety. She smiled at her new friend and thanked her lucky stars once again for this great stroke of good fortune. Lucky things always happened to her in Italy. Something about the air and the color of the light reflecting off of the buildings. In Florence she had spring fever every day.

Fiona gave Simon the message. "There's something wrong," she said. "I could tell from her voice."

"When did she call?"

"About two hours ago. Said she would be in her hotel room tonight."

Simon walked straight to his office and shut the door. The international operator told him to hold on momentarily.

"Pronto," an Italian voice sang.

"I am looking for my wife Jennifer McCall."

"One moment." He was on hold.

"She is not in her room."

"Did she leave a message for her husband?"

"Hold please." A pause. "No. Nothing."

"Is everything all right with her?"

"I assume so, sir," she was offended. "We run an efficient establishment, sir. Everything is taken care of. We take good care of our customers."

"I did not mean. Never mind. Could you please give her the message that her husband called? I am worried about her, and to call me immediately when she comes in. No matter how late it is."

"I will do that."

"Thank you."

Simon hung up the phone.

"Simon pick up on three," Fiona announced on the intercom. "It's the customer from Seattle."

"Thanks," he said and returned to his day's business.

Vincenzo still had a couple of calls to make before he could go home. Not that he went directly home to his family in Scandicci. First he stopped at his mistress's home in the Piazza Santo Spirito. They'd known each other for five years, slept together for four. Like many Italian women eschewing a future of cleaning and cooking for their husbands, she was in it for the excitement.

His whole family knew about Vanessa except for the twins. They were too young to understand, he reasoned. The girls attended art school at the Porta Romana and every night before taking them home, he made a detour to her house to have coffee or to fix something in her apartment, or to make love. She said that he was a kind and passionate lover, though you would never know from the sheets that went flying, the bed that bounced against the wall and the framed picture that once fell off her closet and smashed into pieces. He prided himself on his mistress, loved her dearly, was really in love with her. He told his wife about Vanessa two years ago after she caught him making baby sounds into the phone. That forced him to confess everything, and since she was a domesticated wife with no outside source of income, she could not just pick up and leave. Like generations before her, her mother and grandmother included, she shared her husband with another woman, because she really had no choice. No choice whatsoever. At least he made it seem that way to her.

Vincenzo rang the bell of 50 Piazza Spirito with a thumb that could press a tack into oak furniture. He heard a rumble over the intercom.

"Vincenzo."

"Si." (I will translate the following conversation for you because there was no reason whatsoever for the characters to speak in English.)

"I'll be right down, my love."

"Yes, my angel." People doing naughty things often speak in gooey language, even Italians.

The lovers scurried up the twenty-seven steps through a waiting open door.

"Vanessa, cara, one minute. A problem."

"What is it, my love?"

"There has been a slight change in plans. We cannot leave Friday with the cash. There is an inconvenience." They walked into her apartment.

"What is it?" She fell to her knees.

"Art will not give us the money for the drawing until we do something about this American girl. She has figured it out."

"She has figured what out?"

"That it's a fake."

"How?"

"I don't know. I guess she is smarter than she looks. I don't understand why Art sent her. Merda. We take no chances with her."

"What should we do?"

"Quiet her."

"What?"

"Temporarily get rid of her."

"Kidnap her?"

"We have no choice. Take her up north to your family's place in Vigevano. No one will ever think of looking for her there. In the palazzo your family owns. Could you stay with her for a week? Art promises me forty percent of the deal. We could buy an apartment in Florence. We'll have Jennifer call her husband to say she is delayed and will be home soon. Work. Americans always fall for the work excuse. That is all they do."

Fiammetta and Jennifer entered the club by opening the glass door. A glittering bar hugged them on their right with wisps of fresh coffee floating in the air. The female bartender was blond (not natural) and the male was tall and dark and extremely handsome. They were busy furnishing coffees and cappuccinos and an occasional "long drink" to their customers, many of whom must have been their friends, since both of them were chatting up a storm while doing their jobs, or maybe that was part of their jobs.

Fiammetta asked the guy if there was a lecture here tonight. He said yes and with a gentle arm gesture pointed to a doorway past the bar.

Jennifer smiled. "This looks fun, Fiammetta. Thank you."

They walked through the narrow and low doorway, which clearly must have been there since 1500 when Florentines and people in general, except perhaps those in Reno, were much shorter. Behind it were round tables with three or four people seated around each. Women and men shared coffees and cigarettes and the first reaction that either of them had was about the smoke.

"Gee, Fiammetta. I'm not sure I can take too much of this." Jennifer pointed to a smoker.

"You get used to it after a while, Jennifer," she tried to reason. "No, you don't. I'm sorry, you never get used to it."

"What am I saying? This is your event. Let's just sit down."

They found a table in the back where only one person was seated. She was smoking a cigarette and reading the daily paper.

"Can I get you anything from the bar?" Fiammetta asked politely.

"I'd like a Coke, or Coca, I should say," Jennifer smiled.

Fiammetta left her new friend briefly to return to the bar. This was her chance to check out the women in the café. It would be incredibly tacky for her to do this while sitting with Jennifer. Lifting her head she immediately noticed a slender creature who stood twisted like an olive tree against the wall facing the bar.

"Two Cocas," she informed the female bartender.

"With lemon?"

"Yes, please."

Fiammetta watched as three women walked into the bar and checked her out. One of them even said "Kinda cute," in English. She felt flattered because beneath her tough, poised exterior, she felt insecure about her looks, her hair, and her brains. She overcompensated by being a professor. This way she could be frumpy, smart, and admired. Her parents were brutal to her as a child, telling her she was stupid and ugly.

"Ten thousand lira please," the bartender announced.

Fiammetta laid the 10,000-lira bill on the bar and thought that Italy was damned expensive.

(I will now take the liberty to translate the evening's events for you, my dear reader.)

"Good evening sisters," a beautiful dark dyke said in a lush alto tone. "Thank you for coming to our second in a series of lectures dedicated to lesbian life in Italy. Tonight we have the pleasure of hearing Dottoressa Bettina Vescovo, a psychologist at the University of Florence, who will speak about," she paused to look at her notes, "lesbians in Florence. She has dedicated her life to this subject." (Fiammetta thought that this was a pretty convenient thing to dedicate oneself to.) "She has produced over twenty articles, and one book entitled *Lesbian Life: La Vita Nuova*. Dr Vescovo."

Fiammetta was delighted. She felt part of a larger, worldwide community for the first time. She was curious to see if Italian lesbians behaved any differently from American ones. She was curious to see if she behaved differently around Italian lesbians. Let's face it: she was just happy to be around lesbians, period—especially in Italy.

Dr. Vescovo must have been fifty years old. She was of medium build, about 5'9", had graying hair and a nose that would have inspired Raphael to great heights. It was long, pointy, and brown. Fiammetta watched that nose for a long time and tried to picture it in a Tuscan Renaissance masterpiece she had seen. It was certainly a sign of hundreds of years of breeding. Maybe she was a Medici or a Tornabuoni or a Buonarotti? How great. A lesbian descendent of Catherine de Medici. Fiammetta's blood pressure was rising, even if she wasn't conscious of it.

The doctor introduced herself modestly and spoke in a mezzo-forte tone. Pushing her hair behind her ears repeatedly as she spoke, she introduced her research topic and passed out a questionnaire. It looked like this:

```
Select a number from one to ten. Ten means you
feel this word applies most to you, one that it
applies least.
```

Beautiful	1	2	3	4	5	6	7	8	9	10
Unhappy	1	2	3	4	5	6	7	8	9	10
Faithful	1	2	3	4	5	6	7	8	9	10
Disgusting	1	2	3	4	5	6	7	8	9	10
Perverted	1	2	3	4	5	6	7	8	9	10
Outcast	1	2	3	4	5	6	7	8	9	10
Loving	1	2	3	4	5	6	7	8	9	10
Violent	1	2	3	4	5	6	7	8	9	10
Selfish	1	2	3	4	5	6	7	8	9	10
Lucky	1	2	3	4	5	6	7	8	9	10

She dispensed the questionnaire, and pencils to those without them in their purses. Fiammetta thought this was all incredibly fascinating, even though she did not quite understand the reasoning behind it. Wouldn't straight girls answer the questions in a similar way? How was she defining straight and gay? How was she defining women? How would men react to the same questions?

"This sounds dumb," Jennifer said. "People aren't divided so neatly into straight and gay. Some people are both."

The truth about how Fiammetta was feeling had suddenly been revealed.

"Do I make you uncomfortable, Fiammetta? I mean being married and all?"

"No, no. Yes. I guess so. I mean I barely know you. But hanging around a gorgeous married frightened bi-experienced woman is hard even for the most well adjusted lesbian. It's all so very tempting. Especially in Florence."

Dr. Vescovo interrupted their conversation because she wanted her questionnaires back.

Fiammetta could not look at Jennifer. She just smiled vaguely and waited for Dr. Vescovo's assistant, her lover, to tabulate the results. She was incredibly attracted to Jennifer at this very moment. Wanted to wrap her in her arms and protect her from the evil Vincenzo. Save her. Become the Bionic Woman (her favorite action hero) for an episode of life.

With the results at her disposal, Dr. Vescovo said that this evening's figures seemed to follow those of a study done in Hanover, New Hampshire, four years ago. The figures showed that lesbians have a low physical self-image and high moral fiber. We perceive that the general public thinks we are ugly and perverted, but that we somehow have no choice and therefore give ourselves high marks for being courageous, loving, and determined to live out the life that perhaps was unfairly dealt to us. She made us sound like a community of selfless nuns. Was that the essence of being a gay woman? Ruthless self-deprecation? Had we pigeon-holed ourselves into this role because it soothed our homophobic tendencies like pot, and like pot made us forget the consequences, that we were somehow shortchanging ourselves to the multifarious possibilities of life and sex? We were afraid to live a full life because of the fear of being called names, names that had been hurled at us since our early teen years. This is what Dr. Vescovo was arguing, which, through the smoke and snickering of some in the audience, appeared to make perfect sense to Fiammetta, who couldn't help but nod her approval. She had struggled her whole life to figure out why she was gay, whether it was a matter of being born that way or being ridiculed by her father or smothered by her mother's "love."

She knew that most of the time she disliked herself for her sexuality and wondered if it was natural or if she just had a problem with men as her mother had made her believe. She knew a few things for certain: she felt comfortable with women, yearned to touch women, and fell in love with women.

"I suppose. It just seems much too soon for all this kind of talk. We just met. I don't know you. Why is this happening?" Fiammetta admitted.

"What?"

"This attraction I feel."

This was much too much for Fiammetta to handle. She had extricated herself from a screwed-up relationship that involved a woman and her long-distance fiancé. Ended disastrously (just read *Cauliflower Head*, my novel that will be published soon). The woman never did stop seeing him and wanted to keep the triangle solvent as long as possible. Fiammetta finally broke down and said it was over. Spent the last year of graduate school crying in her room about it. Then got up enough courage to seek the help of a therapist. She has spent too much money in therapy to get involved in something like this again. But they were in Florence together for one more night. Then they would go their separate ways for the rest of their lives, one in Reno, one on the Upper West Side.

"Let's go." Fiammetta finally said.

They smiled at the other women and walked out the door for some fresh Florentine air that wasn't really all that fresh. Jennifer put her hand on Fiammetta's elbow, then slipped it through to the other side. They were walking arm in arm down the street like Italian schoolgirls. How confusing.

When you have nothing to do in New York, you can always get up and do something. You can go downtown, see a movie, go to a museum, hear some music—jazz, comedy. Or maybe just put on your headphones and walk down Broadway. Sit by the river and watch the sunset over Fort Lee, New Jersey. Be nostalgic. New York is a wonderful place for nostalgia because it is only natural to want to escape it. Simon thrived on nostalgia and thought he would go see a movie at the revival house on 95th Street. It used to be called the Thalia until the owner tragically died, and it was shut down for six years. Simon thought he would catch the double feature of *The Godfather Part I* and *Taxi Driver*. He paid the nine-fifty, handed the guy his ticket and walked over to get some popcorn.

"Small popcorn with topping and a small Coke," Simon told the teenager behind the greasy counter.

"Did you say topping?" He hesitated before pumping the metal spout.

"Yes."

Simon watched as the young man filled the basket halfway with popcorn, sprayed some topping on it, filled it some more, and topped it off with more topping. He smiled, thinking that servers never used to make this thoughtful gesture. He retrieved his change and walked into the dark theater.

Simon liked to sit in the last row of the movie house to avoid people sitting behind him. He made these kinds of compromises daily in New York City. I love going to the movies but I have to place myself strategically in order to avoid the weirdos and the kids. I need to take the train downtown, but I can't sit on the bench because a homeless guy has just camped out there and gotten up to go for a walk at the 59th Street Station. I need to get something to eat at the corner store, but would rather order in Chinese food so I don't have to go smell the garbage piled up on the street.

Simon had no trouble finding a seat and was pleasantly surprised because the chairs had armrests with protruding coffee-cup holders. He slipped the soda into the one on his left and dug his hand into the popcorn. The theater was maroon (weren't most of them that color?) and an old-fashioned curtain covered the screen. He looked up at the ceiling to find the old dome painted in stars. Taking in a deep breath, he sank further into the velvet upholstery, put his feet up on the seat in front of him and waited. He knew all the lines from both movies and mumbled, "You looking at me," and smiled. Jennifer would be home soon. Her message said that she was fine. He planned to drive out to the airport himself with a bouquet of flowers. The curtain opened.

INTERMEZZO 3

Press as many Fs, Cs, Gs, and Ds as you can on the piano. Lift up one note at a time, keeping the others depressed for two minutes. Listen.

STORY 3

Fiammetta told her shrink the next story. Her shrink said that instead of parking cars, they should have paid the money and gone to the party themselves.The moral: grow up!

Two Topless Girls on the Beach

Betty invited me to the Hamptons for the weekend to meet rich lesbians. She defined rich as making over $500,000 a year, not over $50,000, which is how I defined it. Mythic girls drove Mercedes, did coke, and hung out on the tip of Long Island. They were out there; but I never really went after them until today, until my friend Betty suggested it, and before I moved out of Manhattan to Oregon of all places.

We met while playing basketball in college. She was the only woman on the team who could clearly go both ways. I don't think that she had an actual affair with Liza, the sexy forward who did the coach's tarot cards on the team bus, but I'm sure she was in love with her. I could tell by the way she looked at Liza on the foul line.

Betty described her new boyfriend to me during the car ride on the Long Island Expressway. Jeff is sensitive; he is OK-looking; he comes from an abusive family; he is in therapy. She said that they met at a bank picnic and that at first he had been incredibly "there" for her. They spent every night together when everything changed. He heard from the Peace Corps. He was headed to Bulgaria in ten weeks.

"Get this. Now he criticizes what I do and what I wear." That was hard to believe. Betty had that kind of beautiful olive skin and long torso that would look good in just about anything.

After listening to Betty for a while, I did what any good friend would do: I spoke about my own problems. I complained about Martha and her photography and how she is so distant at times and how bawdy she is and controlling and horny and talented and of course about my fears about moving to Oregon. As we turned off route 27 toward Sag Harbor, we slapped each other five and vowed to have a good time this weekend no matter what. We were entitled to it.

The house Betty rented with seventeen other people was in North Haven, a small enclave located on a peninsula just before the town of Sag Harbor. A gray contemporary structure built by a Japanese architect and decorated by his Italian wife, the house had four bedrooms, an airy living/dining area, three bathrooms and a washer/dryer, and was furnished in basic blue and white-striped couches and chairs. Cost to rent for the summer season: $30,000. She said it was more expensive because it had a pool.

"Makes sense," I said.

Betty worked in a firm, and I'm sure made a six-figure salary. Not like me, the perpetual graduate student, who still had to ask Mom for a couple of bucks to go to the movies.

Betty told me that we could share the back room with Derek, the hunky investment banker. He was a great guy who stayed out most of the day surfing, swimming, and working on his tan and muscles. Most evenings he showed off what he had accomplished during the day. I said that was fine even though being a "lifer" I hadn't spent a night with a man since I was fourteen and my brother slept in a cot by my bed because his room was being repainted.

"Betty, care for a Coke?"

"Why the hell not."

Then we went to town to have a typical east Hampton dinner: sushi "regular" washed down by a glass of Japanese beer. We watched the fancy cars drive by and discussed which ones we longed for. Betty said that in the Hamptons you always run into someone you know.

While flipping the pages of the South Hampton weekly, we saw photographs of couples at parties in their sporty Laura Ashleys. They were overly tan and drunk. We found features on where to bury your pet and where to get the best car wash.

"See this?" Betty paused. "There's a fundraiser tomorrow night for the Largess Group. $200 bucks a plate," she said pressing her finger to the listing. "They're raising money for lesbian health and legal concerns."

"Worthy cause," I agreed.

The next morning Betty said, "Let's hit the beach." She called some friends who picked us up in a black, late model BMW with a sunroof. They honked their horn, and Betty screamed that they were here and I said, "I know."

Betty told Derek that we were going to the beach. When he asked which one, she said she wasn't sure. He asked when we would be back; she said she wasn't sure. Then he asked us what we were doing tonight; she said that we were probably going to a party but she didn't know where it was or who was having it. Closet lesbians are so imprecise.

Both women looked like they were in their early forties. Sue was dark with plenty of white streaks in her hair. Her eyes were blue, pensive, and corporate at the same time. Short black whiskers sprouted from her upper lip. She wore a baggy T-shirt that read Armani and had a strong Queens accent that said Jackson Heights. Her skin was nicely preserved.

Wendy had a completely different feel to her. She was blond or gray, plumper and very tan, clearly a person who did not make use of skin care products. She had a broad smile, the kind that seemed genuine, though you never know these days. On the first go over, I would say that she was a real-estate person too. She was patient with stupid questions.

We exchanged introductions about who we were and how much money we made. Under my breath, I thanked my lucky stars that I wasn't in real estate but studied art, and though terrified about starting my new life as a college professor, I was still content to spend the next three years—that's the length of my contract—talking about art and life and art and love. They asked me where, and I said, "Eugene, Oregon."

"Risa, my son is just beginning his Ph.D. at N.Y.U. next year. He is enrolled in the English department."

"That's nice," I said blandly about my alma mater.

We made a left turn onto a street that dead-ended into the Atlantic Ocean. Cars were parked in an adjacent parking lot. A man with a white beard checked our parking sticker and gave us a pass. Sue found a spot in the far corner of the lot under some maple trees. Black BMW: don't want to fry on the way home.

We schlepped the accessories to the beach. I took the watermelon-emblazoned umbrella. Betty carried one handle of the cooler stocked with Perrier and Sue the other. Wendy took their two beach chairs.

Not wanting to get too tired, we plopped ourselves close to where we came in. "It's for better viewing," Sue insisted.

Betty spread her towel that had the blue and white Israeli flag on it while I spread out my towel with the Yankees logo. Wendy planted the umbrella and Sue set her Budweiser chair under it. Sue put on her Mets baseball cap and Wendy whipped out the Bain de Soleil #2, and rubbed the grease the color of orange marmalade into her skin. I asked Betty if she had any #8 and she said no, she doesn't burn, why would she? Sue had some.

After covering myself with lotion, I assessed our collective breasts. Sue had rather big round ones with no whiskers. Wendy had practically no breasts—less inviting. Betty had the rather stiff, pointy variety. I fancied saggier models. I have nondescript ones that need a sports bra.

The sun pounded our bodies as Sue handed me the day's *New York Post* and Betty thumbed through *Vanity Fair* with k.d. lang on the cover. Sue read *Business Week* and Wendy had her eyes closed. The beach is quite distracting when you really get down to it. All those waves crashing and sand getting in everything.

Then Dolores came into our lives in a skimpy bathing suit. She was 55—sporting that kind of sandy blond/gray you can only maintain at the salon.

"Hello ladies," she said in a cigarette voice. "We are having a party tonight, a fundraiser for lesbians and lesbian medical concerns. We still need some volunteers. Any of you ladies interested?"

"What do you have in mind?" I asked.

"We need some people to check tickets and collect money at the door."

We didn't think long before saying that we were a sure thing.

"I want you to wear black pants and nice shoes. We will supply the T-shirts. Be at 1254 North Medford Road at 4:30. We'll probably need you until about 10:00. Thanks, ladies." Dolores moved to the couple to our right.

We spent the next three hours frolicking in the water and running up and down the beach.

At 3:00 we asked Sue and Wendy to drive us home because we had to buy some black pants. Skipping some of the boring details, I revved up the Volvo and Betty suggested that we go to Caldors to get cheap black pants. The neon lights inside the store seemed dim compared to the sun's reflection on the beach. Moms tugging on spoiled girls marched by as tired employees replenished the racks with clothes. Betty pointed me to Mecca: young misses apparel. We found two pairs of cotton elastic waistband pants. Her Mom said she always looked better in waistband. We tried them on in the fitting room amidst laughter and a couple of farts. I usually fart when I laugh hard.

The sun turned orange as we made our way to the party, showered, combed, and decked in our new pants and white sneakers. Tall bushes and trees formed fences around peoples' property. No one was about: only an occasional Mercedes-driver. I parked my gray Volvo behind the red Porsche.

"This must be the place." Betty asserted. I stuck my finger in my ear to make sure there weren't any protruding yellow potatoes, as Martha called them. Where is that Dolores?

We walked behind the house where we found an army of people preparing for the evening's festivities. White tables with white folding chairs dotted the manicured lawn like golf balls on a putting surface. Men were busy making floral arrangements for each table. In the house, women were cooking the feast, and one was cutting baguettes.

"Let's get a drink at the bar," Betty said.

I ordered a vodka tonic and Betty had a gin and tonic. The bartender was annoyed.

"She has an attitudinal problem, don't you think?" one of us said. We walked back to the front lawn. There she was in pearls, a flowered shirt, and smart pants.

"We need you ladies to stand in the driveway and make sure that no one parks in front of the house. Tell them to park near the beach." She took a breath. "We are expecting 500 people tonight. I need you two ladies to point them in the direction of those tables. We have to make sure that all the guests have paid and are on the list before they walk into the backyard."

"Sure thing," Betty said.

"One more thing: after dinner we need you ladies to work the silent auction. Barb Cohen will talk to you about that. The guests will begin arriving about 6:00. In the meantime, go find the other volunteers. They'll give you white Largess T-shirts to wear."

"No sweatola," I concluded. She left.

"Why do Long Island lesbians call each other ladies?" Betty pondered.

We walked to the cluster of volunteers and listened to Barb

explain our duties. All of us were to finish our respective jobs at 9:30 and meet underneath the white and yellow canopy to administrate the silent auction. People had donated food, cars, designer accessories, dates with a masseuse; we were supposed to gather the bids written on the brown clipboards, determine who had made the highest bid, close the bidding, and collect cash or credit cards. Blah, blah, blah. The other volunteers were pretty cute, especially Abigail, the labor lawyer.

We went back to the bar to get a few more drinks after the instructions. Dolores sneered at us slightly, but the truth is we didn't want to get dehydrated. We stood at the entrance of the driveway and watched in awe, glasses in hand, as the first carload of guests drove up.

Black Porches with women in them sporting long, blond hair soon followed. It was Oscar night for me: Maybe Jodie or Martina would show up? We told them to park down the block like we were supposed to.

Then we waited for them to walk back up the street and ask us where the entrance to the party was. Betty chatted with every stranger. I stared in delight. Some of the women grinned at me while others snarled because their feet hurt after walking approximately 400 feet back to the house. "Not my problem," I said to Betty.

A stretch limousine provided us with the night's biggest thrill.

"This has to be Sandra or Melissa." I exploded. Out popped three over-processed pretty types from Mount Holyoke or something. Later Betty told me they were pretty bitchy, not wanting to walk across the lawn because they were afraid to ruin their new Valentino shoes. I missed the whole exchange. Dolores was busy berating me because I was greeting the guests with a drink in my hand.

"Just get rid of it." Maybe her date didn't show up.

My anonymous world shattered.

"Risa, what the hell are you doing here?"

It was dreaded Deborah from the city.

"Hey, Deb." I gave her a long hug and stepped back in admiration. "Don't you look beautiful." She was wearing a sheer orange silk pants suit. I'd always wanted to have a fling with her.

"You volunteering?"

"Looks like it."

"Risa, Risa. I can't believe it," Betty bombarded me.

"What?"

"I think I just saw my junior high math teacher!"

"Did she recognize you?"

"I don't know."

"Go talk to her."

She did.

We went back to our jobs for about an hour as five hundred lesbians walked by. Some walked hand in hand, others were more discreet. Some wore designer pants, some designer dresses. Some were in their fifties with mops of gray hair. Some were right out of college. Some came in packs of ten, others came alone. Some looked like Mom, some like Dad. They made me happy no matter how they were. They were my sisters, my partners in this difficult world of being different. We were inventing a safe, cultural enclave for ourselves: staking a claim for our rights to a free and equal existence—in a world that does not include us.

We could hear the PA system in the background and somebody told us that Bella herself was about to give a speech.

Betty said she didn't want to miss it. What about Dolores?

We considered the consequences for a nanosecond.

Back into the backyard we went. While standing among five hundred lesbians with an attitude, we listened to speeches and ate hors d'oeuvres presented to us on platters. Betty passed on the caviar, but I took four crackers in my hand and stuffed one in my mouth. She went for the jumbo shrimp on toothpicks that she dipped in Thai sauce. I took two. I also opted for the deviled eggs, eggplant slivers, and pizzettas. And the prosciutto rapped around a savory breadstick. It's amazing how many finger foods you can stuff in your mouth at once.

"I need a drink," I said in a muffled tone.

We walked over to the bartender. There was some yellow fruit punch in a large glass bowl on the counter donated by the Fruit for Life Company of East Hampton. A card said so.

"Any liquor in that stuff?" Betty asked the bartender.

"No."

"Then make me a Tanqueray and tonic."

"Make that two."

We walked back to the patio to hear other women give eloquent speeches about my health concerns, and how important Largess was and how it was the first of its kind. We were all fighting homophobia that runs as deep as still waters. For the first time in my life I felt that there was somebody or some organization that could protect me from the evil that permeated society. I was ecstatically happy.

On our way back to the bar, we ran into a couple of women we had seen that day on the beach. They were in the television and production business. I was an art historian with my first job in Eugene: Betty—you know the drill.

To our utter amazement, the bartender refused to serve us any more drinks. "Dolores said."

"I am sick of being treated like a couple high school seniors," Betty confessed. Then she said we should dance and pointed to the wooden floor that had been set on the lawn. A deejay was spinning tunes.

"Why the hell not."

I grabbed my friend's hand and led her to a group of well-dressed, gyrating patrons. Betty was a notoriously good dancer. She won the "best dancer" award on all our bus trips back from games. She did have some stiff competition from a swimmer who did a flip down the corridor of the bus; correctly, the judge awarded Betty the first-place prize of all the two-for-one tickets for French fries we had saved from our meal at the Ponderosa. That says a lot.

Seventies music was in and this evening was no exception. We sweated to Gloria Gaynor, Donna Summer, and Rick James. We danced far apart at first, trying out different spins. Betty dazzled me with an array of hand and arm positions. I abandoned my tired moves and mimicked her. She took my hand and led me through some loopy disco steps. We twirled and coiled and uncoiled and stepped on some well-soled feet and stepped off and said sorry and begged for more. The anthem of disco music came on: "Night Fever." Heaven help me. Betty swung me around and around, and the music and lights whizzed by my head as I thanked God or whoever was responsible for giving me my life and for the great time I was having. I sweated caviar and deviled eggs through my Largess T-shirt. I held on to Betty and felt her energy. She slowly lifted my head and moved her red lips toward mine.

I felt a tap on my left shoulder.

"Time to run the silent auction, ladies." Dratted Dolores.

We spent the next half-hour gathering signatures, money, and credit cards. I sold a photograph of a man in drag at Sheridan Square in the Village, a collage of flower petals by a lesbian artist on the Island, and a box covered in blue velvet. Betty manned the fashion station and even bought herself a little number.

"Only thirty bucks."

I was happy no matter what she bought. "It's beautiful."

Dolores growled at us when she came to collect the money. I began to doubt whether we would ever be asked to volunteer again. What could you expect from two topless girls on the beach?

I felt enraptured for the first time in months. We could cope with Jeff and Martha, and not expect things from them that they just couldn't give. We agreed that that was like asking someone to take a lay-up when they couldn't even dribble.

After Dolores kicked us out, Betty took my hand and walked me to the gray Volvo. The moon shined on the old paint as I unlocked the door for her. I cranked open the sunroof to let the moon in. You fill in the rest.

POEM 3

The artist (sister)

Me and my red Ferrari
swerve into the
driveway made cracky by
California poppies.

Slam the door I
get out as Fred, my
brother, leaps

from behind the hedge
to pinch my neck

And ask me if I
like the new photograph
he did of Mom and
Dad because Dad does.

"When are you going
to move out of the house?"
Red-faced and curly-
Haired, I ask him,
a person plum from
cigarette deprivation.

"My new series of
cemeteries in Italy:
square format,
black and white
fake plastic flowers,
relief medallions of war
heroes,
Gray over white, black
creased in off-white."

I locked myself up
and wrote fifty poems yesterday.

I am the artist.
"No," Dad said in 1969 at 5:30.
"My son [Fred]
is the only one in the
family with true artist's
sensibility.
He thinks like an artist."

ART 3

B - B a l l

Vanessa's car was parked in the shadows of a palazzo across the street from the Grand Hotel. She had a walkie-talkie pressed to her ear and wore a brown jumpsuit. A hat, the kind Ann-Margaret wears the few times she goes out in public, was wedged on her head. She listened to Vincenzo's breathing on the other end.

"Where the hell is she?"

"She'll be here soon, my dear." She in turn breathed deeply into the mouthpiece.

"Stop, cara. That's so distracting." He checked his watch again.

"Ten-thirty. Where the hell could she have gone? Wait, I think I see her. She is coming down the street. Damn, she's with someone. Another woman. We have no choice. I'll swipe her away from the other one. Ready. Ready?"

"Yes. Go, Vincenzo, go."

He pulled the ski mask over his head and walked gingerly

toward the two women. As quickly as a mugger in New York City, he smacked Fiammetta on the side of her head with the butt of his heavily ringed hand, pushed a plastic gun into Jennifer's ribs and told her to move. That if she didn't she was dead. Morta, morta. A car sped up to meet him and they were in the back seat of a late model Alfa Romeo. Vanessa stopped ever so briefly to let an old woman cross the road and then she sped off. The license read FI89706, like the last five digits of her phone number, at least that was what Fiammetta saw before she crumbled back down to the sidewalk.

"Signorina," someone was yelling at her. "Signorina." The old woman held her bleeding head. "Aiuto, aiuto!"

Fiammetta vaguely remembers this episode, though how she managed to stop them from taking her to the hospital she cannot recall. She woke up in her hotel room with a hot water bottle full of ice on her head. A young man was sitting by her watching TV.

"Do you need something, signorina? Something to drink? Are you hungry? We are so sorry, signorina. You were attacked in front of our hotel. The guy did not take anything. We have sent for a doctor."

"Jennifer. Where is she?"

"Who?"

"Jennifer McCall?"

"She is gone. Checked out. She is back in New York. I believe. Yes, that is where she is from."

"What the hell are you saying? I was just with her."

"Signorina. She is gone. Home. I assure you."

"Call the hotel manager immediately. Let me speak to her."

She grabbed the phone and started, "Ms. McCall was kidnapped tonight."

"Please signorina. You are not making any sense."

"The guy who hit me took her away. Pushed her into a car. Didn't anyone see it?"

"You must rest, signorina. Your head. You took quite a blow. I wanted to take you to the hospital, but you said no. You would not go. The doctor is on his way. Be still, signorina. Do you want something to drink? A decaffeinated cappuccino, perhaps?"

"What the hell is wrong with you people? She has been kidnapped." She grabbed her head in pain and said, "Oy. I need some aspirin. Yes. Please get me some aspirin." She put the phone down. "Those bastards were serious." Her temple was throbbing. A doctor gave her a shot and ointment and she slept peacefully through the night.

"Hello."

"Simon?"

"Jennifer?"

"Simon. I'm not coming home for a few more days."

"Why?"

"Art needs me to do some more research on the drawing." She tried to smile into the phone with the fake gun pointed at her liver.

"Is everything all right?"

"Everything's fine," she squeezed out, her hands trembling between the silk scarves, her makeshift shackles. "I just miss you. Needed to talk. Listen, call Mom. Tell her I'm fine and that I'll be back soon. I think a few days. Anyway I'll keep you posted."

"I'll call you at the hotel."

"I'm not going to be there for a while. I mean I'm not there now." She felt a poke in her ribs and listened to a whisper in her other ear. "Art wants me to go up to Milan to look at some other things. I don't have a hotel room at the moment. I'll just keep calling you."

He began to talk about work when she interrupted.

"Simon, I have to go now. Sorry I can't talk longer."

"OK. Take care, Jennifer. I love you. Have fun."

"I love you, too."

Vincenzo took the phone away from her face and placed it on the seat.

"That was very good Jennifer. Do as I say and no one will suffer."

A tear filled her eye. Not that they could see it. She was blindfolded as they got on the Autostrada del Sole (The Highway of the Sun).

Vanessa had lived another life before she got involved with Vincenzo: she worked as a translator for her uncle in Florence. Daughter of a German father and Italian mother, she had a slight German accent when she spoke that her friends could only recognize after she had had two or more glasses of beer. She studied a few years of psychology and quit the day after a lecture on Pavlov's dogs because she did not believe that this had anything to do with human beings. She had romanticized psychology to where she wanted it to be about the revelation of the soul's innermost and darkest feelings. She craved for the multiple personalities of the world and liberation of the psyche from its neurotic earthly shackles. Not getting anything like this at school but a couple of weighty textbooks, she stopped and went to Germany for a year to live with her family in Hamburg.

They received her with open arms, this cousin from the land of Michelangelo. Vanessa, a tall slender girl with red and brown ringlets of curls that draped haphazardly over her shoulders, took a job at her uncle's publishing house and during the week edited Arnold Schoenberg's letters. She enjoyed the work enormously, and to her uncle's absolute surprise worked every day from nine to four-thirty—with an hour break—and even half a day on weekends.

He soon gave her more documents, which she edited with the eye of a diamond jeweler looking for imperfections in the stone. She cried when she saw that a period had been omitted at the end of a sentence—and that she hadn't caught it. Until her uncle put a stop to it all and told her that she should return to Italy. She had accomplished enough.

He brought her to the train station on a chilly May day, and each of them gave her a hug and wished her luck. There was not much to squeeze on Vanessa's body. She had lost twenty pounds that year, and only her breasts, which seemed to retain their fullness no matter how much weight she lost, filled the arms of her family. Thank you, thank you, she repeated over and over as she climbed the three tall steps into the first-class sleeper cabin. She walked to seat 351 in the non-smoking cabin, and put her bags in the overhead compartment. She smiled at the graying lady and her dog and moved to the window and waved at her family. Thank you, thank you, she mouthed. Thank you, thank you. She was on her way back home to see the flowers that fell over the walls of the Pitti Palace and the music that emanated from the chambers of Renaissance palazzi. It was the Maggio Musicale in Florence after all.

Simon sat at the window and looked at his view of the Empire State Building. Lavender lights glowed in the Manhattan darkness and reflected off the clouds that hid the moon. If he remembered correctly, the Mayor waged a PR war to have the city pay for these new purple lights to commemorate Gay Pride week.

Sunday was the Gay Pride parade, and unlike the other parades—Thanksgiving, Christmas, Easter—this was one Jennifer and he usually attended. They went to support their friends and to feel good about themselves, and to remember their colleagues and friends suffering from AIDS. They had a common friend from business school, Nick, who was diagnosed just a year ago with HIV. Jennifer's friend from college, Veronica, also contracted the virus from a shady boyfriend in Burlington. It seemed the disease was all around them, even though they were taught by the media to believe it didn't attack the average "normal" person—whatever the hell that meant.

He put his Walkman on and stuffed a twenty-dollar bill into his pocket. Looking for his keys on the coffee table, he stopped when the phone rang. It must be Jennifer.

"Hello."

"Is this Simon McCall?"

"Yes."

"My name is Professor Fiammetta Stern. I am calling from Florence."

"Yes."

"Your wife, Jennifer, has been kidnapped."

"What?"

"Last night a man hit me over the head and pushed Jennifer into a car that sped away into the night."

"Who are you?"

"I told you my name."

"I just heard from Jennifer a couple of hours ago. She sounded fine. Told me she would be back in a couple of days. Her boss called too to assure me that everything was fine and he just needed her a couple more days. Why are you making this up?"

"I am not. I am telling you the truth. She figured out that the Michelangelo drawing is a phony."

He hung up the phone, slammed a Ten Thousand Maniacs tape into his Walkman, and rushed out the door. Too nervous to wait for the elevator, he leapt down eleven flights of stairs into the street light and up Broadway.

Vanessa's Italian family owns a small appliance store in the small Lombard town of Vigevano. Generations of Perolinis have occupied the space, first selling and mending shoes, then moving into the furniture business, and finally to an upscale appliance store. We are talking Italian appliances—designer materials, coffee makers that look like something out of a modern art museum, and knickknacks priced at a minimum of one hundred dollars. The store spans six arches and turns the corner onto the adjacent block, glass filling in the rounded spaces where thick cloth once provided protection. The silver and gold household items glitter in the stoplight window even in the summer because of all the mirrors inside.

Vanessa's three sisters worked in the store with help from their parents around Christmas time. Each were married, and all three lived in the apartments above. In the evening when Giovanna needed more Parmesan cheese, she yelled out the window, "Mamma, I need more Parmesan cheese," and her mother brought it to her within ten minutes. When Gabriella forgot to buy laundry detergent, she opened her window and screamed, "Mamma, can you bring me some soap, please?" Again, the wait time was about ten minutes. Mamma also took care of the grandchildren—two of her daughters had two boys, while the youngest was trying. On alternate days she took the children for walks in the park and mended socks.

The sisters had good educations, each having completed high school, and Deborah, the eldest, even held a degree in architecture. This she used to her advantage, picking up some extra cash by decorating her customers' homes, with items from the store of course. Deborah was the most creative of the bunch, though she had to neglect her imagination for the most part for the good of the store. Each of them worked over fifty hours a week, earning bags of money that they invested in a home on the Italian Riviera near Alassio and a home in the mountains near Lake Como. They also bought a four-teenth-century Viscontean castle on the outskirts of town. They all had the key to the place even though they rarely went there—too depressing.

Vanessa thought that Gabriella was the most beautiful of the quartet. She had eyes like black olives and her skin was dark like Mata Hari's. Her skin's color made Vanessa wonder whether she was a product of their family gene pool; either she was some kind of strange anomaly or her mother had an affair with a Turkish cus-tomer. Gabriella worked mostly behind the register and did the books during tax time, something that in the past she'd tended not to worry much about, since they lived in Italy where paying your taxes was just a suggestion. She met Gianluca in the third grade after his family had moved him to public school, and they married thriteen years later. They loved each other more than any couple they saw, more than her sisters loved their husbands. They were soul mates: never fought over stupid things or complained. Vanessa was quite envious.

Giovanna was the youngest and most sequestered of the group. She was quiet. She liked to play the piano during her free time and even wrote some poetry while passing her requisite hours, usually in July, when the store was empty. She penciled the verses in the borders of account books, and later when no one was around copied what she had written into a diary. She lived a life in her mind and married her boyfriend the way the entire town insisted she should. She was saving money to go to America for a summer. She wanted to rent an RV with Antonio to do the entire contiguous United States, starting in Baltimore, moving south to Mississippi and around to Texas, California, Oregon around to Montana, and then back across. She was determined to touch foot in each state, but as you can see did not have the plan completely worked out. It was mostly in her mind, the way most of her life was and stayed. That is what happens to Italian girls. They stop living life after eighteen. It goes on only in their minds.

Vanessa refused to be a part of forgetting. She preferred to cry in her room alone rather than work in the store and was determined to forgo its monetary benefits. The day she told her family she was going to Germany to work was the day her mother finally gave up trying to change her. "What are you going to do there?"

"Work for Uncle Wilhelm."

"Doing what?"

"Editing."

"And what good will that do you?"

"I want to learn."

"You're willing to give up a steady salary here and for the rest of your life for books?"

"Yes."

"I throw up my hands. Paolo, you talk to her."

Her father, who was a bit more pragmatic than his wife, recognized his daughter's desperate need to go, and without discussing it further, made all the arrangements for her to stay in Germany with his brother.

"Go, Vanessa. We'll see you at Christmas."

Her mother lamented, "You are giving up everything we have worked for. This is our family store. This will be yours when I am dead. Why are you leaving? This is hurting me very much; I feel a pain in my heart. Oh, my blood pressure." This was also her mother's reaction upon hearing the news that at twenty-six, Vanessa was leaving Vigevano, the town of Lombard hunting palaces, for Florence, the home of the Medici. It was a gesture close to treason. It was as if she were moving to another country, and in many ways, perhaps she was.

Her sisters' reactions to the news of her transference were mixed. Gabriella thought it was wonderful, Giovanna felt she was a traitor, Deborah was too busy chasing her rambunctious son that morning to say anything nasty or vindictive. Mamma stopped speaking to her, and her father helped her pack her things for the journey by train the next day. He knew it was the best thing for her. Vanessa wanted more out of life than material wealth, stability, a family, a house, a beach house, a mountain house, a share of the family business; she simply didn't know what it was.

Vanessa finally took the silk Gucci blindfold off Jennifer at a truck stop around Parma.

"Hello, Jennifer."

"What do you want from me?" She awoke abruptly.

"We need to keep you quiet for a few days."

"Why?"

"The Michelangelo. You know too much."

"Who are you?"

"A friend."

"Of whose?"

"Just a friend."

"What happened to Fiammetta?"

"Who?"

"My friend from the hotel."

"She's fine. Don't worry. Would you like something from the restaurant? I was thinking about a cappuccino and a croissant myself. Can I get you anything?"

"No. Why are you so calm? You can't keep me here against my will. I'm going to start screaming." And she did.

"Quiet. Sh. Sh. That is of no use. You can't get out. Get away and Simon will be hurt."

"What?"

"Harm will surely befall him if you try to run. We have contacts in New York. Know exactly when he takes the train to work in the morning, his hours at the gym, and the stores he shops in. We don't want an accident to happen to him. Especially around rush hour. You have no doubt heard of people falling in front of the subway. Gruesome, isn't it."

"You evil witch! Don't you dare harm him."

"It wouldn't be me to do it."

"Where is that slimy Vincenzo? I know he's behind this."

"Enough. Do you want something from the café or not?"

"No. I mean, yes. I would like a prosciutto sandwich and a Coke."

"OK. Do you need to go to the rest room?"

"Yes."

"OK." She pondered the logistics. "We will walk arm in arm like Italian sisters wherever we go. Understand. Understand? Don't try to run, Jennifer. Remember Simon."

Jennifer nodded.

"Wait for me to get my purse. Then I'll open the door for you."

"Fine."

The woman kidnapper amazed Jennifer. She was elegant, probably around thirty years of age, speaking perfect English with a slight German accent. She wore a dark green linen suit. Her hair was red, definitely a dye-job, and her eyes black. What Jennifer would do for her dark, creamy complexion! No need for Lauder products to make up for Mother Nature's deficiency. And that thick hair. Jennifer always had problems with her straight blond hair, which if on the head of a boy of her age would have already been lost. She treasured every strand, arranging it as well as possible to cover her forehead. Her hairdresser told her this gave the impression of having more of it. It figured: her kidnapper was about five-eight, 130 pounds, and nicely endowed. She noticed all this as Vanessa got out of the car to open the door for her.

"Let's go, Jennifer."

She grabbed her hand and slipped it through her arm.

"Where are we?"

"In Reggio Emilia."

"Where is that?"

"North of Bologna."

"We are headed north?" They passed a family.

"Yes."

"Milan?"

"I can't tell you exactly, Jennifer. That would be foolish."

"Of course. Where are you from?"

"Jennifer, please stop asking these questions. I can't answer them." Even though she did answer a couple.

"Yes, I see."

They walked up a flight of stairs to the entrance of the café. This is the big Pavesini stop of the Milano-Roma. Built in the 1960s, it spans the width of the highway—ingeniously—so both the northbound and southbound traffic can use it. The three-star restaurant is located above the road, while the bathrooms and cafés are found in the adjacent towers. Kids with gelati skidded by them, their parents angered by the high cost of visceral entertainment. The two overheard: "Non e' possibile. Venti milla lire per tre gelati."

Both women smiled.

Vanessa found the sign for the women's room and tugged on
Jennifer's arm. She pointed to the right and followed a woman in a
blue dress.

"I implore you. Don't do anything foolish. I have the telefonino in
my bag. I will call Guido in New York right away."

"Guido?"

"Just go."

"Don't you have to go?"

"Already did."

"When?"

"Please stop."

"Yes, yes, of course."

Jennifer walked by the old lady sitting by the door. She was collecting change from the patrons, and snarling at those who didn't
give her a lira. "I am being kidnapped. Sorry I have no change."
What a great excuse, she smiled. Why she was having fun at that
particular moment was not exactly clear. But if she had to be kidnapped anywhere it might as well be in Italy by a gentlewoman
who seemed as if she had nothing better to do.

"Thanks for waiting," Jennifer said sincerely. What a thing to say
to your kidnapper.

Jennifer and her kidnapper walked through the maze of prosciut-
ti, ciocolatini, chunks of Parmesan cheese, olives, and capers to the
banco. The banco is the counter where coffee is served in Italy. It is
Mecca for Italians. Especially it seemed for kidnappers. Vanessa
began to drool ever so slightly after smelling a cappuccino that
crossed her path with an Italian businessman.

"There's nothing quite like a cappuccino," Vanessa said in a
trance.

"I feel the same way. You can't get these in New York. I mean they've recently opened three new chichi Italian pastry places on the Upper East Side. Do you know where that is? Anyway, it's just not the same. Let me tell you. They can't get the creamy part right."

Vanessa was not really listening.

"I do like the ones you can get in the Village. La Bella Villa. Heard of that place? No. I guess you wouldn't. What am I thinking? Sorry. I'm nervous. Mother says I talk a lot when I get nervous. Or does she say, I don't talk when I am nervous? I'm blabbering on."

Vanessa walked graciously in her Valentino shoes— Jennifer recognized the model—to the cashier and asked, in the most delicious Italian alto, due cappuccini, una Coca, e un panino al prosciutto crudo, per favore."

The handsome bartender with a well-cultivated mustache took her money and gave her the receipt, which he then ripped in half when the order was ready.

"Thank you." Jennifer said to Vanessa when her food arrived.

Vanessa nodded and began to sip the cappuccino with eyes closed.

Jennifer was mesmerized. "How is it?"

"Fine. Yours?"

"Good." She went on to herself. "What silly small talk we were making, my kidnapper and me. What does one say? What should we talk about? What the hell should I do in this situation?" Jennifer was beginning to sweat slightly. Her heart thumped louder through her silk white shirt and her thighs in her white pantyhose became itchier.

"What is your name?" Jennifer asked.

"Flavia."

"Beautiful name."

"Thank you."

"Probably not really yours, right. But that's OK. I love your suit. And those shoes. Valentino, right?"

"Yes. How did you know?"

"Saw them in the window on Via Tornabuoni. I really wanted a pair, but when I saw the price, I thought twice and moved on."

"It's quite an investment buying shoes. But they really make the outfit."

"Certainly. I think they are the most important part of the ensemble. Bad shoes ruin the entire look. Italians really understand that. In New York women wear sneakers to work. So as not to ruin their shoes. Amazing. They look so silly."

"I really like your blouse. Where did you get that?"

"Bloomingdale's on Lexington Avenue. My mother got it for me one afternoon. We take shopping sprees together."

"I love the color."

Jennifer finished the last bite of her panino and the two were ready to continue their trip. Jennifer reached for Vanessa's arm and they walked into the chilly air of an Emilian night. She opened the car door and let her in.

"You must place this foulard over your eyes, Jennifer. I know it's rather annoying, but we must do it like this."

Jennifer looked at it and said, "It's beautiful, Gucci? Yes?" Jennifer tied the silk around her head and slumped comfortably in the back seat.

"I feel much better," Vanessa said from the front seat. She pulled out the telefonino and told the party on the other side that all was proceeding smoothly. She said, "buona notte, caro," slammed the car into first, and sped out onto the highway.

INTERMEZZO 4

Billie Holiday's music soothes my spirit after dinner.

STORY 4

Fiammetta first saw Michelangelo Antonioni's *L'avventura* in an undergraduate Italian cinema class. She liked the idea of a main character disappearing so much that she wrote a lesbian version.

Gay Day: Homage to Michelangelo Antonioni's *L'avventura*

My friend Bootsy set me up. She said Amy is "thirty-one, and a really nice, sexy, and politically responsible lawyer." We were supposed to meet on the corner of Davis and 9th near the Nike contingent so that we could march together. I usually march alone with a sign that reads, "Women Who Have Been Mistaken For Men In Women's Bathrooms." This happened to me in Pebble Beach. After I said "I know" to a woman who informed me that I was in the ladies' room, she said, "Oh, I get it. You're here to clean the toilets."

It never rains on Gay Day (or the High Holidays) and this June day was no exception. We were enjoying sunny weather in the mid-80s, which is pretty rare in Portland where it rains three hundred days out of the year. Good for the flowers, I told myself each time I couldn't stand the rain one more minute. Sometimes I drive all the way across the Cascade Mountains to Bend (three hours) for sunshine because the rain makes me all crampy and sad inside.

My life is generally low-key adventure. I am a part-time street musician. I play the recorder and live with my mother, Verna. I dabble in surveillance art: I videotape women who cheat on their partners during backpacking trips in the Northwest. It is a perfect gig for me, because I love to snoop and climb and it helps support my day job. Problem is, as much as I watch my friends' girlfriends doing the nasty near lakes and streams, I haven't had a steady partner in three years and three months. Not after Vanna, the public relations woman with great legs and brains, who, it turned out, was already sleeping with both her male boss and her female secretary. That wiped me out. It figures. I didn't heed any of the red flags: the long weekends in San Diego "with my mother," the late night chats on the waterfront "with my sister." That's when I decided to go into surveillance art. A hobby, really.

I locked my bicycle to a parking meter, pulled out my sign from my left basket, and began looking for Amy. Colorful men with pom-poms blocked my view. Convertibles overflowed with cross-dressers. Children busily gathered condoms that paraders threw into the crowd. "Johnny just asked me what these are for," I overheard a distraught parent say to his wife. A dog wore a sign that read "Proud" inside a pink triangle.

She was leaning up against a car in a denim tank top and cut-offs. Tevas completed her outfit. She was gorgeous from the moment I met her. I walked to her calmly, in a slow tempo, so as not to startle her. "Hey. Amy?" I inquired.

"Harriet?"

"That's right." I couldn't help look her up and down. I said, "Nice earrings."

"Thanks," she shook my hand. Hers was soft like rose petals.

"Like your sign," she laughed.

"Ever happen to you?" I teased her.

She paused for a moment and said, "Can't say it has."

We made some more small talk, even though I was hard-pressed to speak. She was breathtaking and you need air to talk.

I told her I went to Portland State. "I studied medieval music. I even produced a couple of CDs with my group Nuns on the Run." She was delighted. I pulled out my treble recorder from by back pocket and blew a lightning-quick rendition of my signature tune, the English fourteenth-century favorite *Sumer is icumen in.* She smiled. I had her where I wanted her. She was impressed with my intonation.

"How about you?" I asked earnestly.

With some pride and a hint of modesty she said, "I studied law at Boalt Hall at Berkeley."

"Impressive," I said too quickly.

"I'm a legal aid lawyer," she said. "I work with victims of domestic violence." She told me a little about the case of a father who had beaten his autistic son in Tillamook, Oregon. "I helped to move the boy to his aunt's house."

"And you are a do-gooder lawyer, too," I said.

We began strolling behind a group from the local temple Havurah

Shalom, which Amy translated for me as loosely meaning "Community Peace."

I asked her how she knew Bootsy. With precision, she said, "We play tennis together."

"I caught ol' Bootsy on tape cheating on her lover. It was at Opal Creek, near Salem. She was having an affair with the girlfriend of one of my clients."

We'd traded a few more stories about distant friends who might know each other when we heard the mellifluous rumble of the Dykes On Bikes. The parade was starting. I smiled from ear to ear. Gay Day is my favorite holiday of the year, even more than Thanksgiving.

Amy said she was a little nervous about marching because she was afraid that she might run into her ex-girlfriend. I was curious about her past and asked, "What's the problem?

She looked at me in the eye and said, "She had a vicious temper."

"What did she do?"

Amy flashed open her hand in the air and admitted, "She yelled at me a lot."

"When did you break up?"

"A year ago," she sighed.

It seemed a long time to hold a grudge. "And she's still mad?"

"I left her for another woman," Amy said coyly.

"Who?"

"Her sister!" My heart sank a little, but at the same time I felt titillated by the idea.

"Hmmm. Are you and her sister still together?"

"Nope. She left for Santa Fe to pursue a career in photography," she said with an air of finality.

"My history isn't so interesting," I told her. "I had a great girlfriend in college. Her name was Valerie. And that's it. Lately I've been dedicating myself to music and art."

We stopped chatting and began waving to the crowd. A few bookworms lined up behind Powell's City of Books to wave a progressive "Hello." We crossed Burnside Avenue and walked onto Stark Street, the center of Portland's "Boys' Town." Here the parade really heated up. Folks flashed their Bloody Marys at us. Men stood on cars shaking their asses. Women embraced and cheered at my sign. I bowed in approval. We moved toward Broadway, and Amy started asking me about my work.

"How did you know that you wanted to be a surveillance artist?" she asked.

"It's a way to subsidize my music and still remain true to my artistic vision," I said virtuously, knowing that some people cringe when I use the words "artistic vision."

"What do you charge?"

"$150, plus gas, and a blank video tape. I borrow a camera from Portland State."

I wanted to talk more about my artistic vision but she continued questioning me. "What's the scariest situation you've been in?"

"I was chased out of the woods near Mount Hood by two naked women after they heard me outside their tent. They wanted to kick my butt. Usually I set up near their cars and catch them on video kissing. Then I edit the tape at the studio at Portland State. Add some music, change the lighting, cut and paste, add a voiceover if my client desires. After deciding that I like it, I deliver the tape to a suspecting partner. Collect my fee."

She smiled the most delectable smile full of white teeth and fleshy gums, the kind you long to wrap your tongue around.

"Are you a native?" I asked her.

She stopped walking and said, "Nope. I'm from Pittsburgh. Came here to pursue a girlfriend. How about you?"

"Born in Chicago. Mom and I moved here when I was 10."

Suddenly she took my hand. I felt a shock wave. She swung my arm back and forth as if I was her most favorite person in the world. She likes me.

"What do you like to do on a first date?" I asked her.

She blushed. Perfect.

We turned the corner onto Broadway and walked up the street toward Pioneer Square, passing slick retail stores. The sun reflected off windows. Hundreds of cheering people lined the streets behind police barricades. The gay-people haters usually stood here. I was ready for them this year and wouldn't allow their hateful chanting of "Burn In Hell" to cause a tear to well up in my eye like last year. Don't they realize how much they hurt people? This year I don't believe in hell, anyway. I started reading Jewish texts. I recently read Genesis and Exodus because I was longing for a spiritual base. Though my father, now passed away, was Jewish, we never did any Jewish rituals in the home growing up.

Amy's hair touched my bare shoulder and she grazed my behind with hers. Women this beautiful usually have little to do with me. I have a kind of shaggy musician look. Maybe it was the fact that I had started working out at the gym last month. I do sit-ups and push-ups every other day. I also told her some funny viola jokes. My self-esteem was rising like dough. In between chants of "Hey-hey, Ho-ho, Homophobia has got to go," she told me that she lived in the Hawthorne area, Portland's lesbian enclave.

Then Amy kissed me square on the lips for about five seconds—no tongue. I melted. We walked about ten paces and I kissed her back. People cheered. Not knowing what to say, I told her about my lesbian game, the one I play with friends at every reunion of lesbians, be it a softball game, dance, or comedy show.

"Hey Amy. Did you ever play the game where the first person to recognize another lesbian they know wins? Here's the catch. She must know your name (and you hers) and she can't be someone that we both know." This seemed to defuse what just happened. She asked me about some of the nuances in the game.

"Do ex-girlfriends count?" she asked.

"Sure," I said firmly.

Then I kissed her gently. The crowd cheered us further.

A voice called out her name and we both turned around. I had already lost the game.

"Melanie," Amy responded. Melanie had on tight white jeans and a dark blue cotton vest—her arms bulged out on the side. She had a video camera in her hand.

"I'll be right back," Amy said and pranced over to see her. I waited. Then like a cloud moving over the sun in Portland, Amy was gone, swallowed up by darkness. I quickly avoided the oncoming husky Portland Twirlers, propped my sign up against a police barricade, and made my way into the crowd. Through the bodies, I caught a glimpse of Melanie pulling Amy by the hand across Salmon Street. A cop stopped me dead in my tracks. "Wait here. We have to let the ambulance pass." I jumped up and down and watched as Amy moved farther into the distance. After my last jump, she was gone.

Gathering the remains of my imaginary love life, I walked back to the parade, trashed my sign, and thought about what to do next. Maybe that was her ex—of course it was. I began marching down the street with the cross-dressers in high heels. Their sequin dresses reflected my anxiety and their tight butts impressed me. I pulled out my recorder and began to play *Sumer is icumen in.* Maybe she would hear me? Come back to me. I was her Sappho—capable of winning her love through my art. She couldn't have gone very far. A tanned, muscular gal took a video of me playing my recorder. "I am the wandering pre-menstrual," I said to her hamming it up. A sign in the crowd said, "Jesus Loves You," and I thought that was good because I can never get too much love.

"Harrieeetttt," I heard to my left. It was Francie, one of my oldest Portland friends, a charge nurse at Providence Hospital. I ran over to her and put my recorder in my pocket. She was wearing a Lesbian Avenger T-shirt and pink lipstick. Her dark, shiny, straight hair was in a ponytail.

"Oh my God, Francie, I can't believe what just happened," I said out of breath. "Amy, she's beautiful and she's gone."

"Settle down a second." She was great with agitated people. I had told her about my blind date.

"She kissed me and then someone yelled at her and she disappeared into the crowd."

"Weird," Francie said shaking her head.

"No kidding." Francie grabbed me by the elbow and began walking me down Madison Street toward the waterfront.

"Did you look for her?" she asked.

I looked up at her and said, "Of course."

Francie insisted, "Well, what does she look like?"

I explained the dark hair, long legs, denim outfit, thick lips, and mahogany eyes. My voice was progressively getting more agitated.

"OK, OK," Francie said, "Enough. I get it. You're in love."

"Who wouldn't be?"

Francie was a wreck herself, just breaking up with her girlfriend "Crabby Butt," a nickname invented by Francie's friends. Crabby complained about everything, but worse of all she didn't allow Francie to see her friends. She controlled Francie by saying she was suffering from a stomach ache or menstrual cramps or a garden-variety illness. Francie, her devoted nurse, was supposed to stay home and take care of her. No friends for you!

"How are you doing?" I asked my beloved friend.

"Better." She finally told me the news: "I decided to move out next week. Found an apartment."

"That's great news," I said. Crabby wouldn't even let her watch "Friends" on TV at home. She wanted her to watch "Oregon Field Guide."

That's when I saw Amy. "Francie, over there, she's standing near the fountain," I pointed a block ahead of us. She was wearing a red halter-top and striped shorts. I ran ahead, dodged a bus, and crossed the street.

"Amy?" I asked, my eyes focusing shyly on her kneecaps.

No response.

"Amy," I said standing closer. She finally gave me the time of day.

"You've got the wrong person."

I was confused. "What? You just kissed me?"

She clearly wanted me away from her and said sternly, "You might think about leaving me alone before I start screaming."

"What do you mean?" I moved my shaky gaze to her stomach. "You're a lawyer, went to Berkeley. You just told me that."

From out of the corner of my eye I saw three largish women come toward me. One grabbed the back of my neck, while the other two stood at my side. "Leave the woman alone," one warned me.

"Who the heck are you guys?" I asked meekly.

They pulled the recorder out of my pocket and stepped on it. It was plastic so it didn't break.

"Now, did you have to go and do that?" I asked politely, trying to wriggle free of their grasp. They walked me toward the Salmon Street fountain and flung me into it. The water was ironically refreshing. "And don't move," the woman wearing a red shirt and red shorts said. I stood in the murky water with my clothes on and they vanished into the crowd.

"Harriet, Harriet, are you OK?" Francie ran up to me and led me out to the street. I had some duck droppings on my leg. Yuck.

"That was totally weird," I said looking into the crowd for them.

Francie had my recorder in her hand. "Here, take this."

"Thanks." I played a quick rendition of the Brady Bunch theme song to make sure that my instrument was in good working order.

We walked toward Waterfront Park and recounted the events.

"Amy pretended that she didn't know me," I said, pulling off my "Save the Rain Forests" T-shirt and wringing the water out of it. "It was her. I swear."

"Ever see those girls before?" Francie asked me.

"Nope," I swore again and put the T-shirt back on. "Let's walk down to the booths. I want to buy a rainbow collar for my dog."

A makeshift gallery of white tents set up in two rows featured corporate and non-profit goodies for gays and lesbians. The Humane Society brought a den of animals for adoption. We petted a dog named Bubba and wished we could take him home. "I can't have him." I shook my head. "Honey likes her privacy," I said. Francie already had three kitties from the Humane Society.

After I breathed in a whiff of greasy delights I said, "I'm hungry," and suggested a veggie gyro. Francie really wanted to be a "veggie," but had to have meat to make her feel satiated. We walked our drippy food to a booth of rainbow items. Salespeople looked at us warily and I asked Francie to hold my gyro while I sized up a rainbow collar, a pair of rainbow-colored Converse high tops, and a rainbow-emblazoned leather wallet. I like to affirm my sexuality through doodads. After I learned they would not take my check ("we got burned already"), I handed them twenty-five dollars and got some pennies in return. "Want a bag?" the salesperson asked cheerfully.

"Save a tree," I answered.

While Francie went on some more about Crabby, I thought it was the right time to hit the beer garden. They asked me for my ID at the gate even though I was thirty-two years old and my shoulder-length hair was highlighted with plenty of gray. I scurried as quickly as possible to the ticket line, asked for two plastic cups of Budweiser, and paid the woman ten bucks. Francie said she would get the next round—that never happens. We found a vacant white plastic table and chairs, and sat down.

"And she criticizes what I do and what I wear," Francie said, exasperated.

"Tell her to stop," I said, placing my beer firmly on the plastic table.

Francie was notoriously even handed and chirped, "She can't help it."

"Harriet." I heard a slightly familiar voice sounding happy to see me.

"Amy?" I looked up.

"Yes, you remember." She rubbed my shoulders.

"Of course I remember." I said with some frustration. "Do you remember me?"

"What do you mean?"

"You ignored me at the water fountain," I reminded her.

"I don't know what the heck you are talking about." We began to bicker like long-time lovers. Francie began rolling her eyes.

"Never mind, Amy." I put a healthy stop to it. "This is my friend Francie. Francie, Amy."

They smiled at each other and Amy said, "Is this beer for me?"

"I suppose so." I started up again. "Was that your ex-girlfriend?"

"Oh, Mel. No she's not my ex, just an old friend," Amy said.

"She didn't try to hurt you, did she?"

"No." She redirected the conversation. "Francie, what do you do?"

They began to exchange pleasantries and I went to get us some more beer with Amy's money.

By the time I came back, Francie was talking about Crabby.

"She makes you fold her underwear?" Amy asked incredulously.

"And count sheets of toilet paper with each flush," Francie continued.

I suggested we move to a different table because I couldn't stand the wafts of cigarette smoke that were coming out of the circle of nearby baby dykes. Don't they know how bad smoking is for them? I was feeling maternal for my babies. Amy grabbed my hand and I melted. She reached for the inside of my left forearm and massaged the fleshy part. We walked past a woman taking video of the action and I said I was sorry after I accidentally caught my foot in her tripod. She said, "No problem." I reached over and gave Amy a little kiss on the cheek. Beer took over my senses. We heard the MC announce the beginning of the afternoon's festivities and decided to bag the beer cage and catch political speeches and gay talent. The organizers set up a stage on the waterfront before steps that skateboarders usually navigate. Big black amplifiers decorated the plaza and we settled ourselves down on a brick step. Amy held my hand. Francie rolled her eyes.

The events began with some selfless straight political folks fighting for our rights, which was fine and dandy with me. Next up a woman read poetry about her son. A lip-synch artist in gold sequins performed *New York, New York,* as sung by Liza Minnelli. Amy put her leg on mine. Cheerleaders with huge calf muscles did a little *YMCA.* I ran my hands through Amy's hair.

"Harriet, I need to go to the bathroom," Amy said.

"There are some potties to the left of the stage," I pointed.

She got up, and I watched her behind for as long as I could.

"She is so smart," I said to Francie.

"You're weird." She rolled her eyes. "Can't you wait till you get her home?"

"I don't do that kind of thing on a first date." I paused. "You're just jealous, anyway."

"Shut-up."

After a social worker gave a rendition of *These Boots Are Made For Walking,* a punk band from Bellingham, Washington, called the Dri Heaves came on stage. It featured three women in ripped clothing and leather boots. Their music sounded like colliding hubcaps. They sang lyrics like "Homophobic bastard." It was refreshing— really. I was a little tired of the day's messages, like people marching with T-shirts that read, "Straight But Not Narrow." And the Nike contingent throwing Nike balloons and candy into the crowd. And the politicians in sporty casual clothes asking for my vote. Remember when gay pride meant angry Act-Up folks demanding change? Remember when gay pride meant topless women with buzz cuts and tufts of underarm hair? Remember when men paraded in leather thongs?

Francie and I began to groove to the raucous beat. The green-haired drummer pounded on her instrument. "She looks sort of familiar," I said to Francie. "Didn't she toss me in the fountain?"

Francie thought a second and said, "I can't tell."

We cheered when they finished *Bigots Belong In Hell.* We got up to dance for *Kiss My Mohawk.* Then the drummer announced a special guest singer, "Screama," from Portland. The crowd was quiet with anticipation.

"Oh, my God," Francie said. "It's Amy."

"What?" I adjusted my eyesight.

She was wearing two rainbow stickers on her nipples. She had on tight black jeans and pink lipstick.

"Cool," Francie said.

Amy screamed into the microphone at the top of her lungs and danced around in a tight circle. I believe the lyrics were "Die Gay Basher," two octaves above middle C. She ran around the stage and beat her hands on the drum set. Then she kicked the amplifier, which must have hurt. People cheered. She spun her head around in convulsions. She fell to the stage for a second and got up to the heavy thumping of bass drums and guitars. We stood up and cheered her on. The music came to a halt on a low C. The band dropped their shoulders and there was silence.

"Wow. She was great," I said honestly.

"Kind of weird," Francie added.

"You're just jealous," I said, nuzzling up against my friend.

We waited for her to come back so we could tell her how great she was, but just as before, she disappeared. Francie said it was better this way because things were happening way too fast and she thought the whole thing was kind of weird. We sat through the Gay Choir's rendition of *We Shall Overcome* sung in six-part a cappella harmony, and we listened to the spirited performance of *Both Sides Now* by the Portland Lesbian Choir. I walked over to the ice-cream vendor and bought two coconut chocolate swirls.

"Thanks," Francie said, never even making a move for her wallet—typical—and droned on, "When I was sick last week and it was pouring, she [Crabby Butt] made me walk to the store to get medicine."

"She didn't!" I said loudly.

"I swear." Francie shook her head. "She didn't want me to waste gas."

The dance started as the sun began to hide behind the hills. An African-American DJ spun tunes. Children, older folks with no tops, tree-lovers, and people of all shapes and colors got up and began shaking their groove things. He played some favorite seventies stuff, and hip-hop to the delight of folks under thirty. I felt empowered by the crowd's diversity. This was a different scene from the one I had stumbled upon in Chicago a couple of years ago. I was in the Windy City taking in a recorder conference and decided to march with a friend. At the end of the parade we walked to the usual booths of gay paraphernalia and found that the celebration was boring and monochromatic. I suggested that we head over to Lake Michigan and put our toes in the water. We strolled under a roadway and into a vast expanse where many African-American families had set up tents and barbecues. I thought we had walked into a big celebration party. And it was. It was a huge Gay Pride. Men were dancing with men, women with women. It was loud and smelled great. We danced and wondered how our community could be so splintered. Our rainbow flags can be misleading.

We danced for about an hour and decided it was best that we go. Can't have too much of a good thing. Anyway, I had to go home and get my gear together for the next day's shoot at Ecola State Park on the Pacific Ocean. A friend wanted me to do a video of her on the beach playing with her dog. Francie walked me to my bicycle and told me she was taking the bus home. I gave her a big goodbye hug before she boarded the bus and told her I would help her move. I put my recorder in my bike basket and unlocked the U-lock.

Someone tapped me on the shoulder.

A sexy voice said, "One last embrace for the camera?"

I turned around to find Amy, Melanie, and the three women who had hauled me into the Salmon Street fountain. Amy grabbed my hand, positioned me in front of a nearby music store sign, stared me straight in the eye, and said, "I can't see you anymore." Then she kissed me.

Melanie pulled out the video from her camera, put it in a plastic case, and handed it to me with a smile. I looked at it and said, "What do you want me to do with this?"

"It's a little present from Bootsy," Amy said and walked away.

"Can I see you again sometime?"

She just kept walking.

POEM 4

Road Trip

Hunched over the wheel
accelerate through the
curve.
You are so stupid!
Put your shirt on.

Little yellow flowers line
the road home.
Burger King one hour
and twenty minutes
Bear (my soul) Mountain
left
at Route 4.

I know Grandma liked her
she made her eat so much.
And Mel the week before
And the night on the floor
And the day on the lake
And the night on the bed.

This week: look for an
apartment, practice, write
Mamma, play hoops, party
Thursday.

But I like it when she
honked the horn
while I was driving
Stop Gwen, no go
No stop, no Go.

I should have gone to the
bathroom before I left.
Scarsdale exit 21
You were exit 42.

Would you chuck the
friggin' cherry pits out
the window?

ART 4

A Bad Girl's Tenure Decision

Fiammetta dumped her luggage on the bed and walked into the kitchen. The flight wasn't all that bad considering she had to change planes at London-Heathrow, wait three hours for the connection, and sit next to a spoiled twenty-year-old English son of divorced parents who said he flew to New York whenever he had nothing better to do. At least the cab ride back to Manhattan was pleasant. The driver was Polish and knew Vodka, a painter friend of Fiammetta's family.

Fiammetta opened the refrigerator to see if there was anything to eat. A piece of salami lay on the metal rack and next to it some Evian water. It was tempting but Fiammetta figured she probably shouldn't eat more salty stuff, given the six packets of salted peanuts she ate on her flight. She found a grapefruit in the drawer and decided that would probably do, pulled out the cutting-board, a dish, and a pointy knife. Carving grapefruits was one of her favorite pastimes because she could daydream about other things and still feel productive. The side of her face was fairly swollen and it felt good to put the cold grapefruit on it.

"Oh," she winced. "How am I going to explain this? No one seems to believe me." She spoke to the grapefruit.

Fiammetta thought it was a good idea to visit her parents in New York before making the trek back to Reno. She hadn't seen them before her flight to Italy because they were on Mackinac Island. They were a close-knit family (a metaphor these days for dysfunctional) who depended on each other for happiness. Mom was Italian and Dad Jewish, which was probably the beginning of her troubles, though she wasn't really ready to admit it. They provided her with a good education (N.Y.U. for graduate school, Vassar College for undergraduate) and a safe home environment (no alcohol or drugs) but didn't pay enough attention to her problems or feelings. Vincent, her brother, was an artist who lived in Brooklyn. He was a nice fellow and of all her family, he accepted her homosexuality with the most ease. He said that was because many of his art teachers in college were gay or lesbian and he respected them the most.

Her parents were naturally a different story. Dad, a retired ad executive, pretended her friends were just friends and wasn't it nice that Fiammetta had such interesting ones at that. Mom, a capable housewife, was completely baffled by the revelation made when Fiammetta was nineteen, and thought her daughter ought to think about hormone therapy—too much testosterone was Mom's diagnosis. Upon further examination, it seemed that Mom's biggest problem was the fact that Fiammetta insisted on being open about the unnatural state of affairs. "Why must you tell everyone?" she asked her daughter not too long ago.

Fiammetta heard someone unlock the front door. She wiped her mouth and walked to greet them.

"Mom, Dad?" she yelled in the family tradition.

Mamma looked Fiammetta up and down, "Skinny. A little skinny. Everything all right?"

"Yes, well sort of." She walked toward her Dad.

"What is that on the side of your face? Clara, did you see that? Nini, what happened?"

Mom panicked and switched on the hall light so she could see better.

"I got mugged in Florence." Another round of gasps and Oh-my-Gods. "I'm OK. I'm fine. Didn't break anything, no stitches."

They walked into the living room and flipped on the light.

"What did they take?" her father asked.

"Nothing."

"What do you mean nothing? What did they want?"

"They didn't want me. They wanted my friend Jennifer."

"Aren't you hungry?"

"I just ate a grapefruit."

"Do you want me to make you some spaghetti?"

"No."

They talked a bit more about the events in Italy. Mom wanted to know about the prices of things and if she had bought herself any nice shoes. Had she at least been to the Uffizzi? Had she met any interesting people? Had she seen the David? They did not speak about the lesbian conference. Mom would be disappointed. Life can be so lonely for a lesbian speaking to her parents. Fiammetta felt empty at this moment and thought it better that she get some sleep.

"How long till you go back to Reno?" her father wanted to know as she cleared the bags off her bed.

"Two days. I leave Thursday. Classes begin Monday and I want to give myself a couple of days to regroup."

Perhaps moving to Reno was not the worst thing.

Simon decided to go to the company softball game after all. They played in Central Park around 66th Street once a week, and though he had skipped the last two games, he thought it best that he show up this time, at least for team support. By the time he reached the fields he noticed that his team was already warming up, so he ran, mitt in hand and cap on his head, to the bleachers. The unofficial coach was busy penciling in the lineups.

"Good to see you, Simon," Ralph said raising his head. You're in center tonight."

"Fine, Ralph. I'll play wherever you need me."

"We need you in center. Tough game tonight. The lawyers from Smith and Bromwell. They're at the top of the standings."

"What are we?"

"Five. We have to beat them if we want to make it to the play-offs."

"Right."

Simon gave his keys and his wallet to the coach and jogged out to center field, which is like no center field in the world, facing straight into the heart of Manhattan, the flashy buildings of 57th Street providing a barrier to the taller ones sprouting up behind them. The sun reflected off the diagonal line of the Citicorp building and the Plaza Hotel's old spires fought for a spot in line. A hot dog vendor held court to the right of the backstop and some homeless men were on the green bleachers. Everywhere Simon turned something amazing was happening, and as he was lost in the visual barrage of stimuli, he didn't notice a ball hit out toward him that almost knocked him in the head.

"Shit." He scampered to get it.

The grass he ran on was sparse and, amazingly, didn't smell like grass. It did not have any smell at all. He tried to think of other natural things that don't smell, but honestly couldn't. New York City grass is like a war survivor; it has all but its most vital qualities beaten out of it, but still stands.

Simon bent down to pick up the ball in as macho a way he could muster, reared back, and fired a bullet to the first baseman, who, as in the other games, dropped the ball. Simon wasn't quite sure why they put someone on first who always drops the ball, but he figured that Coach Ralph must have tactical reasons. Simon stood in center field flanked by Nancy the real estate appraiser in left and Toni the ambitious account executive from Dallas in right. Simon knew he really was pretty good for a mediocre player.

Ralph called everyone to the bench and read the line-up to cheers and squeaks from the team and supporters.

"Fiona playing shortstop and batting clean-up, Simon center and batting fifth." Fiona played on her college team in Staten Island and was, if Simon was not mistaken, an all-American. Is that right? Anyway, she was about five-ten and 160 pounds, had long dark curly hair and gorgeous, strong biceps. Simon had only seen them once in their full glory: the time they had attended a wedding together. Team Chase Manhattan, with powder blue uniforms and a white C on their caps, huddled together and said, "Hustle team," and sent Doug from Pension Funds to the plate.

"All right. Let's go. Pitcher's got nothing," coach Ralph said along with other assorted softball-related jargon used to inspire and intimidate.

Fiona got up and walked into the on-deck circle, which in this case was not quite a circle, but a patch of barren turf. She swung the bat around her head and flexed it behind her back and knocked some dirt out from her cleats and then did the whole dance again. She adjusted her cap and redid her bun to make sure all the hair was in it. Her biceps were growing with each stretch and gyration, and Simon, himself a lifter, was impressed.

Simon watched as Fiona took a strike at the knees and glared at the umpire. She called for time and stepped out of the batter's box, which from years of neglect and the digging of thousands (could we say millions?) had become a trench. She stepped back in after she found her composure.

"Wait for a good one, Fiona. Hang in there. She's got nothing." Coach barked. Pitch number two was a ball.

Fiona sent the next pitch over the head of the woman in left. Granted, it seemed as if the woman was taking a short siesta but Fiona hit it so hard that it flew over her head like a fighter jet, and by the time the outfielder had readjusted her hat, Fiona was rounding second and gracefully heading for home. A two-run inside-the-park home run (the only kind possible in Central Park), and Simon greeted her at home plate with a smile. Fiona gave high fives all around.

Simon scratched more dirt out of the trench and settled in for his turn. He looked at a ball, then a strike, then a ball, having trouble being assertive and just going for it. He stepped out and looked at Ralph.

"Good job Simon. Hang in there. Wait for it."

He got back in and swung at a pitch in the dirt.

"Shit."

"Shake it off. Shake it off. Simon."

Simon shook his head in disgust. He got down on himself easily.

The next pitch was a call strike three. Simon tossed the aluminum bat at the backstop and flipped his plastic battering helmet to the ground. "I suck," he mumbled to himself.

The C team took the field to a smattering of clapping and to the yelling of George the deranged softball fan, who had hobbled out from his living space underneath a bridge in the park to take his usual spot on the topmost rung of the bleachers. He was an outpatient from Bellevue and everybody knew that he was harmless, just incredibly annoying. Wearing the layers of clothes that he had been collecting for decades, he sat and yelled at the players in a tenor coloratura for the duration of the game until Ralph or whoever was coaching walked over to him and handed him some money so that he could get a bite to eat. Then he left and returned a few minutes later, hoagie or hot dog in hand, ate, swallowed, and began to yell all over again. Then someone bought him a beer. And so it went, until the game was over. A solitary pigeon wandered in front of Simon. The nerve.

Jennifer found herself blindfolded in a cold place. It was dank and musty, and when Vanessa finally took the damn thing off her head she couldn't believe her eyes, because she was seated in what looked like somebody's living room. A huge vaulted ceiling hung over her and she looked directly into a fireplace framed by oil paintings and hung rugs. A wall-kitchen was to her left and expensive wood furniture filled the other side of the room. A Persian rug covered part of the wood floors, and antiques, the kind movie stars collect in their spare time, were leaned up against the walls. Art deco lamps sat on bookshelves and on a writing table. Stroking her leg was a fluffy black cat with green eyes that looked as though it had access to the best grooming in town.

"Where are we?" Jennifer couldn't help herself.

"I can't answer that."

"This feels like a castle."

"It is."

"Where?"

"I can't tell you that."

"Oh, of course."

"The refrigerator is stocked with goodies. There is plenty of wine here in the cupboard to keep you happy." Vanessa strolled over and pointed to the stash. "Have as much as you like." She paused. "The bathroom is through that door." She pointed to a huge dark wooden frame. "Shampoo, toothpaste and brush are in there. I use Pantene. Hope that's OK?"

"Fine."

"I've taken the phone away, and there's no sense in screaming because no one is around. You are in the country. Only the birds can hear you and they won't help. The TV is there, and wait, let me get you the remote." She searched under some pillows and the black apparatus fell to the floor. "I'm going to make myself an espresso. Want one?"

"Yes. Flavia, what do you do for a living?"

"I edit."

"What?"

"Music books."

"How interesting."

"It is really. I've done it for many years."

"Funny—I just met this really terrific musicologist in Florence before I was kidnapped."

"Musicologist? I am sorry for you. They are so pedantic. At least the ones I have met. Rather a sorry crowd."

"Not this woman. She was actually a lot of fun. We went to a lecture together before I got kidnapped."

"That's nice."

"A lecture about lesbians in Florence. It was quite an experience."

"Don't know any. Wait. Wait. I did have a friend who knew one."

"Who owns all this art?" Jennifer pointed to the wall.

Vanessa poured the coffee into two blue and white porcelain cups. "My aunt Francesca. In the summers she opens the downstairs to visitors and uses the space as a gallery. She has quite a collection of Barni. Ever heard of him?"

"Nope."

"A wonderful Florentine artist. Sugar?"

"Yes."

The women kept talking like this for what seemed hours. Vanessa told Jennifer about her sisters and the family store. Jennifer told her about her meddling mother, and her beloved husband, the most devoted, kind man on the planet. At one point, Vanessa brought out a salami and some regional bread and over a glass of Barbera they ate sliced bread and salami before moving on to some marinated artichoke hearts. Jennifer felt comfortable with her kidnapper. There were few options in Italy for women besides getting married and having a family, Vanessa explained. Vanessa was one of the few single women her age—let's say 30—in Italy who wasn't a widow or divorced. People treated her with a certain amount of disdain. She made her married friends uncomfortable. This freedom. But the truth is, she wasn't alone; she did have somebody. She had a male companion who loved and took care of her. Came to the apartment to fix a light fixture or install a smoke detector. Vanessa dined at his family's house and saw his kids grow up to be teenagers. Bought them gowns for the Italian equivalent of the prom. In the end she kept her freedom, her freedom to be whomever she wanted, not tied down to washing somebody's underwear or socks for the rest of her life. For this she had to suffer in different ways.

"My family doesn't approve of my lifestyle. They want me to leave him and find a real husband. I would rather die."

"I have always done what my parents wanted. College, business school. I married a nice guy from business school. Never really rebelled. "

Jennifer and Vanessa had exhausted another avenue of conversation and it seemed that as hard as Jennifer was stalling, it was time for Vanessa to leave.

West End Avenue looked different to Fiammetta that sunny afternoon. She'd forgotten how the sidewalk sparkled and how music could be heard from the windows of buildings she passed. Grownups on fluorescent roller-blades scooted past her, and occasional owners of short, long dogs strolled along. Fiammetta's piano teacher Dmitri lived on this block; she took lessons from him for three years until he sat on the piano bench with her and told her to hold his hand as he demonstrated the proper technique. That was crossing the line if she ever experienced it; she canceled the next month's lesson and finally broke with him completely. He was married with four lovely kids, each of whom was making TV commercials and print ads.

She walked to 84th Street and into the building marked 500. As was customary before she moved to Reno, she pressed the buzzer marked Dr. Lorraine Bittner and waited for the hissing sound to announce she could enter through the glass door. She waived to the elevator man seated in the corner reading the *New York Post* and walked down the long, marble-floored corridor to a green door.

"Damn, I'll never remember it." She looked desperately at the combination lock that required her to punch in three secret numbers. "Fuck." Then the door opened. Lorraine stood in all her Bolton's (or perhaps Loehmann's) splendor (nicely outfitted, but a touch tacky).

"Fiammetta, I figured you might have forgotten the number." She let her into her office. "It's great to see you." She gave her former patient a meaningful hug.

"I've missed you, Lorraine." They walked by the waiting area with its array of highbrow magazines (the *New Yorker* for starters) and into her studio. Fiammetta made her way to her usual spot at the end of the flowery blue and green couch and the doctor sat on her leather chair. The room was decorated with tasteful reproductions from the Metropolitan Museum of Art and kids' plastic blocks and a board game filled the floor. Fiammetta looked up.

"Tell me everything about your new life out there." Lorraine said in her heavy Brooklyn accent.

"Where do I begin?"

"The job. Start with the job."

And she did. About her annoying colleague who was hitting on her and the orchestra director who was a complete goofball and the wonderful student who brought her a rose on her first Valentine's day in Reno and the cute but loony Spanish professor whom she might have a crush on. She told her about the new Toyota Corolla she bought instead of the sexier Fiat and the house she was renting six miles from school. About her bitchy landlady who must be a recovering alcoholic because she is so anal about telling Fiammetta where to park the car and put her garbage. And how she spends her free time listening to music and going hiking with a friend or two. That was all she had so far. She had no love life to speak of out there. Though she did manage to meet a nice woman before she left for Italy.

"Why don't you call her?"

"I'm leaving in two days."

"She sounds like she would make a good friend."

"I suppose." Fiammetta hesitated and then said, "I met someone I like in Italy. Jennifer. She was kidnapped."

She told her story for what seemed to be the thousandth time.

"Forget about it. You don't need that in your life right now."

Lorraine spoke to her in the same (s)mothering tone that she did before Fiammetta went to Reno, and this both comforted and upset her. She did not want mothering at this moment, but rather a patient ear. Her love life was in its usual state of disarray. She jotted down Lorraine's suggestions:

1) Stop calling your ex-girlfriend Stephanie. It's over.

2) Do things for yourself. Plan fun time.

3) Your mother is not going to die from her high blood pressure. She's under a doctor's supervision.

4) Find a basketball team to play on.

These tips seemed rather minor, but to Fiammetta they also meant that somebody cared.

Time was winding down and Lorraine said, "I'm sorry we have to stop now." Thankfully, this one was free. A friendly visit, a touch up. Maybe she would see Mary of the Hong Kong Movie Theater after all. Made sense. She walked to the first unoccupied, working pay phone she could find (this took her about twelve minutes), called information, and got Mary's number.

"Hello."

"Mary?"

"This is Fiammetta."

"Hi," she said in a voice reserved for lovers. Fiammetta was sure. "Welcome back. It's great to hear your voice. What are you doing today?"

"Nothing really."

"Come down. Let's hang out if that's OK."

"Sounds good."

"Can you come down in an hour?"

"I think I can manage that."

"Bye," Mary said slurring the syllable in warm anticipation.

"See you." That wasn't hard at all.

She walked up to Broadway and into an independent bookstore. It felt good to be home.

Simon was pissed. He went 0 for 4 with a walk and an error. He couldn't hit a thing. He was inconsolable. Ralph had tried briefly. But of no use.

"I stink. God, I stink."

"You got a couple of good swings in there."

"I should quit. What's the use? Then to see my secretary, my own secretary, belt two over the left fielder's head. I can't take the humiliation."

"Come have a beer at Julian's Pub."

"Nah."

"Jennifer's still in Italy, right?"

"Yeah."

"So come on."

Ralph led his team out of the south end of Central Park, through the parking lot of Tavern on the Green and onto Central Park West. Fiona was cooing at her friend and the ambitious right-fielder was chatting up a storm with Stone, the new Harvard MBA on the block. Simon walked up to meet Mel, their drop-the-ball first baseman. He was safe.

"Hey, Mel."

"Hey, Simon. Nice game."

"What do you mean? I stunk out the joint."

"You made a nice catch in center. That was a tough ball."

"I guess." He couldn't get himself to return the compliment. He just couldn't. Mel dropped the first three balls thrown to him. Cost them three runs. He seemed to settle down after a while, but he still caused most of his teammates to feel frustrated, especially Marc, the hotshot shortstop who threw his mitt down in disgust. Maybe that was cool after all. Yeah. Simon liked the fact that Marc got angry.

"You made some nice plays over at first." Simon shook his head. "Some really nice plays."

"Thanks. I have trouble seeing the ball sometimes. You know I'm blind in one eye."

"No, I had no idea." Simon started to feel awful.

"Lost it when I was five in a boating accident. I won't go into the details. Unless you want me to," Marc smiled.

"No, that's OK. God you play great. I mean for having only one eye. I mean, forget what I just said. You play great in general."

"Not that great."

They both smiled.

Columbus Circle opened itself up to the softball players like a tulip. A statue of Columbus stood pointing to the sky in the midst of six skyscrapers that formed its petals. The statue is placed so high on its pedestal that no one ever really looks at it, or even remembers that it is Columbus. People really don't care much for his figure in a city whose many residents have been oppressed in the Dominican Republic, Cuba, and Puerto Rico. Good thing he was so far out of reach. He could get hurt.

The group of about eight players waited for the lights to turn green (and sometimes crossed when they weren't green) as they made their way around the circle. Homeless people lined the side- walk in front of the New York Convention Center selling used pornographic magazines (you can just imagine what was on some of the pages), old shoes, scratchy LPs and other household items. One man even had what looked to be Simon's leather jacket that had been stolen three weeks ago from a restaurant he had gone to. A family sat on the corner and the mother asked for change. Simon bent over and handed her the contents of his softball uniform pocket, which was not very much. She god-blessed him as the children continued to play with a rope they had probably found in a back alley. A hot dog vendor with a red and yellow cart made a sell, as did the pretzel guy to his left. New Yorkers were feeling generous that hot summer evening. Wasn't this the best time of the year in the city? Simon thought so as they headed into the pub on 57th Street.

Ralph waved hello to his friend the bartender and motioned the team to find a seat in the back, near the jukebox and away from the spearing motions of the guys playing pool. Simon and Mel grabbed some chairs for the eight players and they all settled in around the greasy, mahogany table. Fiona was still chatting feverishly with her friend to the point that she tripped over the legs of a bar stool, knocked into a man cuddling a pint of Guinness, said she was so sorry and kept on going as if nothing happened. She pulled the chair out for her friend and asked her what she wanted to drink. A Coke. That sounds good. Both of them did not feel like drinking tonight. Simon ordered pitchers of beer for the rest of the table and waited for the bartender to fill the musty plastic containers with liquid that looked like the suds from his dishwasher. Thanks. He paid the twelve bucks, grabbed a handful of mugs and settled them down on the table. Then he went back to get the other three glasses.

"What do we owe you, Simon?" Ralph asked.

"Get the next round," he said in the manner he had learned from his friends. Seemed believable.

"Aren't you drinking?" Mel said when he saw Simon reach back to the bar to retrieve something red.

"No. I don't really like beer."

"What's that?"

"Cranberry juice and soda. Want some?"

"No thanks. I'll wait for the beer."

This corporate crowd did what most do in New York City: got drunk and talked. What else is there to do in a bar? There was watching a game; the Yankees were up 3-1 in the seventh against the White Sox. Simon watched several innings with Mel. There was playing pool; but who was going to ask those three enormous guys with tattoos if they could join in? There was looking at the pub decor, something that did intrigue Simon—and he noticed that the motif of this particular place was baseball caps. Every inch of wood around the bar was covered with dirty baseball caps decorated with college team insignias, logos of trucking companies, professional teams, and corporations, and images of bare breasts. Each hung on a hook and moved slightly when the door of the joint opened. Baseball caps were particularly manly for some reason, perhaps because they cover bald spots.

"Jennifer's in Italy closing a deal on a Michelangelo drawing."

"Really."

"Sounds a lot more glamorous than what we do, huh?"

"I guess."

"She's staying an extra couple days to finish. Want to know something funny, Mel?" He paused.

"What?"

"Some strange woman called me and said Jennifer's been kidnapped."

"Weird."

"Did you get her name?"

"No."

"I hung up on her. Thought it was a prank. I had just talked to Jennifer ten minutes earlier."

"Have you heard from her since?"

"Yeah. Everything's fine."

"People can be such assholes for a laugh."

"Nothing better to do."

INTERMEZZO 5

Sing along to Puccini's "O mio babbino caro." Do it a second time while taking a shower.

STORY 5

Sometime during her twenty-four years of schooling, Fiammetta learned about witches.

The Good Witches of Porciano

While staring at the ceiling, I imagine the guy riding the noisy Vespa scooter veering off the road and flying into the Arno. And the man revving up his diesel-powered truck at the Piazzale Michelangelo swearing to me that he will never start it again. How can I experience the white and green beauty of Santa Maria Novella amid all this dust and noise? And for what? For a blissful week in Florence, during my winter break, with my friend Miriam the Good Witch of Porciano. Whenever I feel lost, Dad tells me to write

Miriam a letter explaining my predicament. This time he thought I might as well go to Florence and visit with her. Get a little free direction.

Miriam lives in the Santo Spirito neighborhood, near the Pitti Palace and away from what we usually think of when we dream of the city—the Duomo, the Palazzo Vecchio, or the Uffizzi Gallery. Yet rather close to the Ponte Vecchio, if not that close. She has lived in the same fifth-floor apartment for twenty years. Miriam recently had work done on her fifteenth-century flat, which initially housed Carmelite nuns. A well-tailored architect updated the kitchen with bright red appliances to go with the original Tuscan terracotta tiles. He added a second floor by bashing through the ceiling and finding new space under the roof. He later put in a skylight.

Miriam gets up every morning at 7:30 and fixes herself some toasted bread with a healthy dose of green olive oil the color of the Arno. Her capped teeth crack into the bread. She follows this with a splash of strong American-style coffee—I think she even owns the German equivalent of a Mister Coffee. Brushing the crumbs off the table and onto the floor, she says she'll wash the dishes later. Housework is obviously not a priority for this witch. Why should it be? "I live alone anyway," she tells me one morning. "Besides, the lofty spirits do not care about mildew, soap scum, dust, or a bathtub ring." She says something about hiring a woman to come tidy up. She always speaks in English to me even though I am fluent in Italian because she feels best communicating to me in my native tongue.

Nothing Miriam wears betrays her powers. No crystals hang around her thick neck. No glittery rings adorn her fragile fingers. No frilly cotton shirts festoon her skinny frame. (I had met a witch in New York City sporting this type of shirt.) She looks professional every morning, opting for form-fitting suits or tight dresses. Her hair is not particularly big (another trait of witches, I think), cut neatly to about ear length and clearly a product of repeated visits to the salon. It has a beige tinge, a favorite of Italian coiffeurs. She is average height: not too small like a witch or two I had seen in a store window in Little Italy, or too big like an Amazon I read about in junior high. Her legs are good, straight, covered today by a long, black skirt. Her upper torso, with small breasts, is disguised by a white turtleneck that emits the slightly stale smell of overuse. And except for those strange eyes, which take on a reddish glow in the light of a Tuscan late-summer afternoon, I don't think you could tell that she is a witch. Nope.

Each day she joins other Florentines on their motorini, illegally crossing "no vehicle zones" to get to work. She goes through as many red lights, cuts off as many pedestrians, and curses the traffic as frequently as the average rider, arriving at her office in the German National Library dirty and sore at the back of her neck where she keeps all her tension. My father met her by chance in the library one afternoon over a cup of coffee. They became fast friends after discussing an oil painting he'd bought in Woodstock, NY, from an antique dealer. Dad thought he had discovered a long lost Ingres. "What do you think?" he asked. Miriam searched her stars and responded, "Yes, yes, I sense it is an Ingres."

Her job as secretary to the library director does not interest her particularly. It is a steady paycheck and not much of a hassle, except at the end of the year when she has to put together the annual report. She leaves the job punctually at 5:30, without ever eating lunch, and makes the trek home on her gray and blue Garelli model. That's when the day really gets under way.

The phone begins to ring at 6:00. One patient from Milan has a terrible ear infection.

"Think of why you have it," Miriam says. "Why do you wish for an ear infection?"

After some back and forth I hear, "Stop talking to him on the phone and it will go away." (The woman calls back two days later to say the pain has miraculously subsided.)

To the woman who has such terrible arthritis in her fingers that she can no longer play the piano, Miriam says, "Why do you wish this upon yourself?"

Then she hangs up the phone obviously frustrated and says to me, "I can't do anything for her. Her pain results from years of strangling her children for attention. She says she can't live without them. So needy."

We spend a little time examining my own problems. I am in my second year of college and frustrated. "Will I get a good job when I graduate? I'd like to be a writer, but I worry whether I am good enough to make it. I am also having trouble meeting people. Spending too much time alone." I complain about my low back pain.

"Why do you think your back hurts?"

"Bad posture."

"Why else?"

"I never exercise."

"You worry too much. Just be yourself and your pain will subside." She got up and moved her hands in circles over my head. And paused.

"You will feel better. And you will publish a novel."

Lately there is more serious business to attend to. Her good friend, Deborah, with whom she has discussed the secrets of healing for over ten years, has been diagnosed with brain cancer. The disease has set up residency from her brain to her toes, and her doctors have given her two months to live. One rainy day in a Roman hospital, Miriam told the specialists not to begin chemotherapy because it was of no help and wheeled Deborah out the door past the incredulous staff. She brought her friend to a Sardinian beach. They sat and looked at the stars and worked with the energy of the universe, the energy that according to Miriam permeates every moving body. In Miriam's philosophy, the same force that brings disease can heal it. Disease is part of life, she tells me: a challenge, like changing a tire on the Firenze-Roma highway or filling out tax forms the night before the deadline. It is a time to take responsibility for one's own life. "Only good can come out of disease," Miriam explains.

Each night Deborah calls Miriam to tell her about the bleeding, the blindness in one eye, the vomiting, and the loss of feeling in her toes. This is eight months after her departure from the hospital, six months more than she is supposed to live. Miriam talks to her in a soothing yet stern voice. "The seizure is a good sign. It means your body is fighting back." There is no desperation in her tone. "Don't give up."

After the evening's set of phone calls, Miriam eats spaghetti, drinks a glass of local red wine, and goes out. Sometimes she goes to the movies (where she always cries, even during *Dirty Dancing*), or an aerobic workout in the studio by the Porta Romana. Most of Miriam's work is accomplished in the middle of the night. Before falling asleep and while sleeping, she meditates "astrally." She thinks about the relative placement of the stars and, through her new skylight, fixates on orbs and constellations that are connected to healing. Galileo Galilei, a great healer and astrologer, is Miriam's mentor and friend. She speaks to him all the time. Last night they talked about Donatello's bronze David in the Bargello Museum. Miriam is writing a scholarly article about the work, but confesses to me she does not think anyone will publish research by a "spiritually-trained" art historian.

One morning Miriam says she is very tired and admits, "I am doing my best," over her first cup of coffee.

Then the phone rings and she exhorts her friend by telling her, "Courage, have courage. You can do it." The voice does not answer her. After getting off the phone she shakes her head and acknowledges, "This is going to be a very difficult case. More difficult than I could have ever imagined. But if we can do something, if we can succeed, it will be a great victory. I will change the way the medical establishment deals with cancer." She raises her fist in the air and flies out the door to work. I collect my passport, guidebook, and sunglasses and leave to see Donatello's David.

One night Miriam takes me to visit her mother, Rose, in Porciano, a little town some forty kilometers northwest of Florence, in the direction of Pistoia. Porciano sits above the city of Vinci, the home of Leonardo, the great painter and scientist. Miriam derives much of her powers from a huge oak tree that shades a church on a hill in Vinci. "Leonardo sat under the tree when he was a boy." She will bring me to the tree so I, too, can experience the benefits of its ancient energy—maybe next time when she is not so busy.

Rose has lived in Porciano for nearly fifteen years. She is about eighty and resides in a cold, damp apartment on the first floor of a eighteenth-century Tuscan villa. Like her daughter, she has worked her whole life. Upon retirement age, she opted to be alone, the ideal condition for a witch.

Every morning Rose walks two kilometers up the hill to fetch water from the medieval well. She needs the special water for her brews because Rose heals with potions rather than with stars. She leaves water on the windowsill to absorb the energy from the sun. Then in the spirit of some early twentieth-century healers, one by the name of Bach, she mixes the sun water with different herbs she picks from her garden. Each "situation" calls for a different brew: basil for high-blood pressure (a popular ailment), lavender for hair loss (not so popular in Italy), oregano for poor self-esteem (popular with me), and sage for lack of sex drive (N/A). I think she uses the leftover water to boil her spaghetti.

Miriam visits her mother every two weeks to make sure she has enough wood for the stove, food in the refrigerator, and company in the house. They do not speak much when they are together, and I gather that witches are people of few words—especially around guests. They are too busy trying to figure out—through fixating on energy—what the heck is troubling their visitor/patient. Everyone's problems are fair game for witches. On Saturday Rose looks me up and down and asks me if I want a cup of tea and a piece of toasted bread with some delicious virgin olive oil. "No thanks. Maybe later," I respond politely.

Rose is not Italian. She speaks with a German accent that makes her roll her R's and sh her S's. She grew up in Berlin. Her father was a psychiatrist and her mother a nurse. She is a foot shorter than her daughter, with straight gray hair and gray eyes. Limping slightly, she walks across the kitchen to put away her deck of cards. Witches like to play solitaire. It helps them relax. So Miriam told me. She also told me Rose has had a difficult life, separated from her Italian husband at twenty-nine with a small child. She was forced to find a job when every other girl in Italy was busy "doing the house."

Rose never did return to her native Germany because it depressed her. She loved the orange sunsets and olive-covered Tuscan hills.

So she made ends meet as a translator and gave tours of the Uffizzi on the weekends, when it was more crowded. I can tell that Rose is a woman of enormous strength because from the moment we walked into her kitchen she never nagged her daughter about anything. Not even about something as universal as her hair. Or the fact that she is single.

They discuss Deborah's severe illness this visit. They speak in English because I am present.

"She feeling better?" Rose asks.

"No."

"What do you think?"

"Nothing seems to be helping."

"I can make her a tea. Can you bring it to her?"

"Sure. Anything. I will take anything you have at this point."

"How is her family?"

"Crazy. They can't stand to see her so sick." She pauses. "Her husband passed out the other day. They are worse off than she is."

"I'm so sorry."

"Nothing to be sorry about," Miriam says nervously.

"And you. How are your fingers?" She takes them in her hand.

"Bad. Bad. This cold weather certainly doesn't help." She lays her fingers flat on the table to reveal their yellow tips, the color of a Cadillac.

I touch them: like a metal railing in winter.

"Miriam, you must see a doctor," I say, concerned about my friend.

"I have. There really isn't much to do."

"Can't you take anything for it?" Bad question.

"I don't believe in ingesting unnatural potions."

"But this is serious." Another poor point.

"So is cancer."

The rest of the evening is spent talking about Bill and Hillary and their first year in the White House. They are not big on the First Family, especially Bill who in their eyes is two-faced and vindictive. What about his Bosnian double-talk? First he says America will intervene, and then nothing. And the issue of gays in the military (I am impressed by their range of knowledge). Rose defends him slightly on his efforts to penetrate Asian markets.

"I don't understand why the Europeans don't follow his lead."

I tell Rose that I am going to Paris next fall on a college overseas program.

"Oh, I adore Paris," she says.

"When were you there?" I ask.

"In a past life. With my husband. He was a banker."

Not much else is said that evening. Miriam is anxious to get back home to check on her patients. I never do drink my self-esteem brew.

"Good night and pleasant dreams. Do you remember your dreams?" she asks me.

"Not really." I lie. This is not the time.

Miriam drives us back to Florence in her speedy Fiat. I hold on to the sides of my seat for dear life as she tailgates trucks and whizzes by a slower-moving Mercedes. She accelerates to red lights and curses pedestrians for crossing her path. Finding a spot near her Santo Spirito apartment is an adventure. After circling the narrow streets for over twenty minutes, she finally comes across something that might work. She gets out of the car, picks up a red motorino and moves it to the other side of the street. She rearranges a bicycle that is leaning up against the sidewalk and shoves a trash can. She sizes up the space, nods her head, declares, "This will work," and backs the Fiat into this infinitesimal spot.

"Can I get you some tea?" she asks me after we walk into her apartment.

"No thanks. I'm going to sleep early."

"Is everything all right? You seem a bit anxious tonight."

"It's all this sickness. It's really difficult for me to hear about your patients."

"This is my mission. I do my best." Then the phone rings.

"Hello," she says in the most dulcet tone. Like Orpheus's song, it could entrance the guardian of hell.

I wave good night and go to my room. It is dark and time for her to work. I listen to any sound of hope as I undress and quietly brush my teeth. Miriam reassures her friend that things will be better. "Courage. Courage." She shuts off the lights and walks to her bedroom under the moon.

My eyes affixed to the ceiling, I recall every detail of what happened today. When my self-esteem crystallizes, I will write a story about Miriam. In the meantime, I pray that her astral work helps her friends in need.

POEM 5

Zoe and the Little White Dog

In honor of Mark Tucker
The gray invitation read 7:30 meet
at the Lutheran church on East 54th Street

He encouraged my frail pen to write
when thoughts to paper produced fright
and all I wanted was to be with her.

She was this or that girlfriend of my obsession
stealing me away from my dreamy profession
to be a writer of little known stature.

Ten people spoke of his dedication to jazz
academics, students, brother, with grim pizzazz
followed by the pianist who played with leisure

An improvisation on *Tis a Gift*,
as the angels in flight gave us a lift
knowing Mark was in music's hands to nurture.

After the ceremony we went to a reception
in the penthouse of a Park Avenue mansion
to mingle, eat, and drink wine for pleasure.

His wife Carol, and two kids, Zoe and Wynn
received condolences gracefully again
with red eyes from watching Mark suffer.

Mark died at forty-six in his tenured prime
a taciturn man, lost in the sublime
of Duke's orchestrations and the juncture

Of jazz and classical music styles,
he had even written some about Miles
for a legacy lung cancer was destined to puncture.

His daughter of eight reached for a cookie
and crouched down to give it to Snookie
the little white dog sniffing her sweater.

Mark's spirit did not attend the memorial—
too serious, sad, and ceremonial.
He was under the table singing to his daughter.

ART 5

Gladiator

Fake Roman Gladiator Asking For
Rome April 30, 2001   QUARTERS

Jennifer was awakened by the sound of the door opening.

"Good morning," rang Vanessa's voice.

"Hello," she responded sleepily.

"What do you say we go shopping?"

"Are you kidding? I'd love to."

"You've been in this room for four days. No sunlight. Let's go."

"Do I have a choice?"

"Get dressed. I am going to take you to Valenza, the gold jewelry capital of Italy."

"I thought Florence was."

"They sell it in Florence, but make it in Valenza."

Jennifer jumped up and made her way to the shower. "I won't take long."

"I'm in a good mood today," Vanessa yelled into the bathroom.

"Why?" Jennifer shouted back over the dim of the falling water.

"The deal, she is settled."

"Already?"

"Yes. You go home tomorrow. We have our cut. No problems."

"I suppose I should be happy for you, but you are after all a criminal, and I am the victim." Those were Jennifer's last words before she jumped in the shower.

Vanessa took this time to snoop in Jennifer's purse. She found a picture of a skinny, dark, and compelling face (must be Simon) and one of an older, distinguished-looking woman (must be her mother). Jennifer also carried a change purse, her passport (not a bad picture really), and a full supply of Revlon make-up. Some postcards of Florence, keys, and a rabbit's foot rounded out the contents. She put the purse down, picked up Jennifer's sweater, and put it to her face. She liked that smell very much. Jennifer's perfume, what was it? White Linen? Something definitely Lauder. She liked her clothes, too. Especially that suit she wore when she was kidnapped. It was something American, but looked snappy anyway.

Jennifer walked out of the bathroom completely dressed. Like a dog that hasn't been taken for a walk in six hours, she marched right to the door and waited for Vanessa to open it.

"Let's go."

"Aren't you going to bring money?" Vanessa asked.

"You're really serious about shopping?"

"Of course."

"I could get something for my mom, I suppose."

"Or Simon."

"Maybe. He never brings me gifts from his business trips."

Jennifer walked gingerly back to her purse, afraid that if she left the door, Vanessa might change her mind about taking her out.

"We've contacted your boss and he knows you're returning tomorrow. Simon has been notified about your flight. We made all the arrangements. We drive to Milan tomorrow morning."

"Fine. I'm anxious to go home. Not that this hasn't been great. Really. Don't get me wrong, Flavia."

"Let's go."

Vanessa showed Jennifer down the dark stairs and onto the ground floor. Thick stone lined the corridor and she saw fluorescent lights gleaming from adjacent rooms. The door of one read Agenzia Brianzi.

"What's that?"

"My family rents the space out to a local real estate guy."

"And that?" She pointed across the hall.

"A graphic arts studio."

Jennifer had not come in contact with direct sunlight for days, and when it finally hit her in the eye she winced. It was the brightest, sunniest day she could remember. The sky was blue, the color of cheap carpet. The light bounced off the castle and back into space. Bright green trees waved at her in the wind and the breeze funneling down the main street met her head on. Two lovesick birds flitted before her eyes and gravel got stuck in the web of her sneaker sole. Life had stopped for her briefly and was being jump-started like an old Alfa Romeo. Once it finally did, Jennifer embraced the elation and skipped toward the street.

"I forgot about all this."

"You what?"

"I'd forgotten about all this movement, and color, and action." Vanessa grabbed her by the wrist as though Jennifer was an unruly child.

"I'm sorry we had to do this to you." This was the first time Jennifer had heard any remorse from her abductor.

"What do you want me to say? Don't worry about it? It's OK? No hard feelings? I'm still horrified."

Vanessa unlocked the door of a red Fiat Uno.

"Maybe shopping will help." She paused. "I just never thought I would like you very much. You seemed like the typical spoiled American when he described you." She put the car in gear and they inched onto the main thoroughfare. "I want to apologize. Really. I am sorry. We just had to do it. Here, take the telefonino and call Simon. Tell him in your own words you will be on British Airways flight 590, arriving New York tomorrow night at 9:00 P.M. Go ahead, call him."

Jennifer dialed up the home number and left a message on the machine. She didn't feel like tracking him down at work.

"I'm so sorry," Vanessa began again.

They drove through sleepy Lombard towns whose claim to fame was their rice fields, and stopped at a lone traffic light in the town of Lomellina Po to allow the oncoming traffic to pass. The road was so narrow that only one direction could flow at a time. The town was semi-deserted, hugging the ancient highway with boarded-up windows and the neon of an occasional beauty salon or conven- ience store. Kids circled on bicycles as angry mothers called them from their windows to come eat. Christmas decorations that had gotten stuck to the buildings billowed in the slight breeze. It was hot that morning, especially in this prehistoric valley in mid-Italy where the Mediterranean had once flowed. Seagulls still floated about the town scavenging for food, in the same place where fish once swam. It was sticky that morning, stickier than any sticky summer day on Broadway. Jennifer was sure of that.

Windy roads marked the transition between Lombardy and Piedmont. It was a subtle change in landscape, but nevertheless a crucial one. Clumps of poplars began to fill the horizon. Towns were not as narrow; many were rather new, rebuilt after being completely destroyed during the war. Apartment buildings, most with balconies of four to five stories, comprised the residences of Ivery, and strip malls, lines of luggage, shoe, grocery, and furniture stores had taken the place of the contado, the Renaissance land holdings of the rich Piedmontese. In the distance the tops of the Alps could be seen.

The Piedmontese were mountain people from France, the Lombards lake people from Germany. A rather crude way to differentiate the two, but that's what Vanessa said, and Jennifer believed it. Vanessa said that Vercelli, a town in Piedmont, bred the most pedestrian people in Italy. They did not have a thought in their heads. Like the poplar trees that huddled in groups, they sat around aimlessly together at cafés and restaurants (she was referring to the men) and talked soccer and hunting. They were not a tribe of people who worked. But worse, they were boring, boring like the ladies playing cards on the boardwalk at Atlantic City. Just the worst. Vanessa once worked in Vercelli because of its proximity to Ivrea, the home of the famous late medieval Ivrea musical manuscript. She edited an introduction to its colorful pages, which contain some of the most beautiful Gregorian Chant of the period, but never met an interesting person in those six months.

They spotted the first sign for Valenza Po and smiled at each other. It was only eight kilometers away, and they both acknowledged a feeling that was triggered by the thought of shopping. Not unlike salivation at the smell of food, shoppers experience an increased pulse rate, sweaty palms, and a bit of ecstasy (the biological reason for this escapes the writer) at the thought of available merchandise. They sat at the edge of their car seats, eyes poised for the sign of the first jewelry shop. Sure enough, on the left-hand side, before even arriving into the town, Vanessa noticed a shop in the midst of a strip mall.

"There," she pointed triumphantly.

She pulled the Fiat Uno into the left lane and waited for what seemed an interminable amount of time to turn into the parking lot. They each locked their doors and got out. A sign read Gioielleria Ponti. Perfect. Jennifer was the first to peer into the glittering vetrina. Rows of rings with colorful stones were propped up on red velvet platforms. Underneath them lay bracelets and still further down the necklaces. Each item had a tiny price tag attached. Most of the lira amounts faced them. Sparkling mirrors heightened the entire scene. Jennifer took a large breath and pushed her face as close to the glass as possible. Vanessa did the same. They did not speak for several minutes.

The owner of the store came out to help. That is customary in Italy. It is impossible sometimes to just window-shop. Vanessa said that they were just browsing and didn't need him at the moment. Jennifer was mesmerized. And the prices! Much better than in Florence. She would say a third less. Her blond hair reflected the jewelry back at itself. Gee, that ruby necklace would be great to wear out. Price: six hundred and fifty thousand lire. That's not as bad as it sounds. It's only about three hundred dollars. And the bracelet. Do people still wear bracelets? They do on Long Island. Jennifer would even wear that gold and emerald one. She might feel awkward (aren't bracelets a bit tacky?) for a bit. But it wouldn't matter. This one was from Valenza and she could save money. It was fairly understated as bracelets go. Thin, made of linked filigreed chain, crowned by an emerald. She could definitely go for something like this.

Vanessa's reaction was less intense. She wore bracelets and gold rings as a matter of course (Vincenzo was after all a generous man when it came to his mistress). In fact, she was thinking of purchasing something for Jennifer. A gift to say that she was sorry. Perhaps it would ease Jennifer's mind, or perhaps more correctly, it would ease her own.

"Which one do you like?" asked Vanessa.

"That bracelet. The one with the emerald."

"Yes, that is beautiful."

"Let's go look at it."

"I think we should go into town and look at the other shops. In Italy when you walk into a store it means that you are ready to buy. There is no such thing as browsing inside the store."

"I know that." Jennifer paused and pulled her face away from the glass. "Let's go."

They jumped back into the car and cranked down the windows. It was hot that morning right before lunch. Vanessa took Jennifer to the center of town where she parked the car in the train station parking lot. They walked towards the shop that Vanessa knew, the shop of her father's friend, Signore Pozzi.

"Here we will find something. I guarantee."

And they did. Jennifer picked out a thick, twisted gold ring she wore on her third finger. It gave her a feeling of power the minute she put it on, the way she felt in a pair of cowboy boots or wearing a leather vest. And something for her mom. Something not too expensive, a skinny necklace perhaps. Simple, understated but still in gold. A chain. Not a necklace. Signore Pozzi helped her find the perfect model. Finally, something for Simon. She looked and looked. Jewelry is not particularly popular among American men. Simon would never wear a ring or a bracelet. There is always the tie clip. He would wear a charming and debonair Italian tie clip. Pozzi found just the right one. Vanessa did not move during this entire process. Just nodded her head slightly each time Jennifer said, "Do you like this one?" The ultimate companion shopper.

It took approximately twenty-five shopping minutes to choose what she wanted, which in real life felt more like forty-five. When Jennifer reached into her purse, Vanessa grabbed her hand and said that she would take care of the ring. She wanted to give it to Jennifer as a present.

"You must be feeling guilty," Jennifer said.

"It's not about guilt. I want to give you something to remember me by. I'm not sure we will ever see each other again, and I have had such a great time with you. Please let me."

"Go right ahead."

Vanessa paid for the ring, which Signore Pozzi put in a blue velvet case. Jennifer used her credit card for the gifts and asked that he place them in cases and wrap them in paper with a bow. They walked back out into the muggy Piedmont air and decided to get some lunch. All that shopping can sure wear a person out.

Fiammetta crossed town at 14th Street. It was either that or 12th, and today she felt like being a part of the new New Yorker scene, something she missed in Reno. She watched a group of men play three-card monte on top of cardboard boxes with two unsuspecting midwesterners. The men fled when sirens were moved up Broadway, leaving their boxes behind. Asians sold plastic scuba divers that crawled along the gum-dotted pavement and pretend cellular phones. Shoppers left stores with bright pink bags overflowing with tacky purchases. Dominicans scratched slabs of ice and poured syrups to make delicious summer treats. Fiammetta avoided some drunken men swearing on the street. Ah, home!

She turned south down 5th Avenue toward Washington Square

Park. She had many beautiful memories there—for instance the time she and her college friends smoked pot in the park and got kicked out by the police. Or the time she vomited after an extended stay at McSoreley's Pub. Or the times she watched the flame-thrower or the unicycle guy. She passed the New School and remembered her uncle's memorial service there some three years ago. He taught writing for over thirty years when he wasn't hanging out with W.H. Auden or John Cage. Uncle Mel was a true Village intellectual of the kind recently replaced by upwardly-mobile business school types. He was also the first member of the family to whom she came out and he probably, in retrospect, saved her years of acting out and self-destruction. The day she told him, he gave her a hug and took her on a tour of the gay people and establishments he knew in the Village. They went to the Oscar Wilde Bookshop where he introduced her to the cashier and they walked to the "gay" pier off Christopher Street to look into the depth of the Hudson River as other gay people lounged about, busy working their tans. He said that being gay was like being a flower: God made gay people and flowers.

Deciding she didn't want to keep Mary waiting, she turned east on 12th, forgoing Washington Square Park for now. The memories weren't particularly worth the detour. Then she came to the Strand Bookstore, where she could not help but walk in. This was one of New York's jewels, an enormous space filled with used books, stacked high to the ceiling. Just a few minutes, really. She walked through the grungy turnstile and smiled at the check-in people who made sure she did not walk out with a bag full of books (without paying). She smiled at the guard, who smiled back. She smiled at an elderly man hunched over a bin of dollar books and again at a young woman and her daughter browsing the children's section.

She turned to walk out with her book fix, and still smiled. This was what she loved most about New York City: the multitude of people all doing their own thing and not bothering you.

Mary's loft was on the corner of 9th Street and 1st Avenue. She'd lived there for the last eight years, four of which were spent trying to evict her upstairs neighbor who practiced the drums at all hours of the day and night. Mary went ballistic each time the drummer began her exercises, stomping upstairs and banging on the door: "You'll pay for this Rita, you selfish pig. You'll pay." But Rita never did, and Mary expended a lot of energy writing letters to the land-lord and the housing commission to no avail. Rita just went on banging on her drums, and sometimes, when she wasn't doing that, walking across the floor in clogs or spiked heels. Just to spite her, Mary thought.

When not bothered by the drumming, Mary was a pleasant indi-vidual: caring, loving, and very attractive. She ran her own birthday card business from her loft. A small color TV stood before the couch so Mary could comfortably watch the Weather Channel for reports, or gather interesting meteorological tidbits. She usually drank sun tea while chatting with clients or friends and had several crawling plants in her windows. Stacks of prints lined her bookshelves, and pictures of her family filled frames. This is all Fiammetta remem-bered from the night they had spent together.

It took at least three minutes for Mary to answer the front buzzer, at least that was Fiammetta's experience to this point. When she didn't answer after the first long two minutes, Fiammetta didn't panic. Mary poked her head out of the window and said, in the most friendly, affectionate voice imaginable, "I'll be right down." She wasn't right down.

Fiammetta sat on the stoop and faced the sun. Kids played basketball in the cement yard and hollered at each other after a bad play. Kids were more vicious these days. They carried guns and regularly appeared on the six o'clock news. Mary came down smashing. Her dark curly hair hung over her shoulders like an expensive shawl and her icy blue eyes, the color of an alpine crevice, met Fiammetta head-on. She was wearing a customary white T-shirt and Bermuda shorts, both with surfing logos, and had a tan from weekends at the Hamptons. She hugged Fiammetta with all her might.

"I'm so glad to see you. I'm happy you called."

Fiammetta shrugged, slightly taken aback by Mary's sudden beauty.

Mary grabbed her arm and led her down the block.

"What do you say we get some ice cream?"

"Sounds fine." Fiammetta was still rather subdued.

They filled each other in about the events of the last three weeks. Mary bought a used ten-foot surfboard. She got up on the board for the first time last Saturday afternoon, and had the bruises to prove it, which she showed Fiammetta when they sat down at the outdoor café. Fiammetta was very impressed, especially by the bruises that women surfers get on their hips because they are women and must lie on the board. Mary said something about feeling the board push up against her pelvis like the thrust of a lover each time a wave passed beneath her. She spoke of the symbiosis she felt with the ocean as it lapped over her and said the water made her feel like she was still in her mother's womb. Fiammetta was starting to get turned on by this surfer stuff.

Mary told some stories, one about a model who fell off the Central Park carousel during a photo shoot. Whenever her family ate ice cream they melted it down with their spoons and called it dead-bunny soup. Sometimes Mary found her cat in the refrigera-

tor. Fiammetta told her about meeting Jennifer who disappeared
into thin air. She could not explain it. No one believed her even
though she had a bruise to prove it. Come and gone like the babe in
Antonioni's film *L'avventura*. She is the star at the beginning, in love
with a handsome dark man (if Fiammetta remembers this correctly),
and they go to an island on vacation with a bunch of friends, and as
Fiammetta explains, the woman vanishes. She is not to be found
and he falls for her friend, and the rest of the movie is about their
love story. Might as well have been about dead-bunny soup for all it
seemed to matter now.

It was Mary's turn to tell another story, this one about her life in
L.A. The time she was sunbathing nude (stoned) in the backyard of
her father's Malibu mansion. A rubber ball came bouncing over the
fence and she got up to give it to the little boy peering over. Ten
years later this same boy asks her sister Julia out on a date. They've
been seeing each other ever since.

"I told you my favorite family one about my uncle who gave me
a driving lesson across the Alps?"

"Yeah, I love that one. Tell it again."

"Really, you want to hear it again?"

"I'd love it."

They went on like this for at least two hours, exchanging ideas
and morals, perspectives and smiles and a few tears at times. When
Mary told the story of her mother's heart attack and Fiammetta of
her Uncle Mel's tragic last days of cancer they both sobbed. Then
they laughed about the Hamptons party. They recounted a couple
of juicy ones about ex-lovers. The check came and Mary held
Fiammetta's hand.

"You are beautiful, you know that, Mary. Don't you?"

"I suppose I do. But tell me again."

Vanessa took Jennifer home to meet the family. They were expecting her at some point, since Vanessa told them that a friend from New York was spending a week at the castle conducting research using the Visconti family archives. Vanessa briefed Jennifer on the story and said that the afternoon was the best time to meet everybody because the shop was closed and the kids were asleep and her father was not quite so rambunctious. She drove into the center of Vigevano and parked the car next to the portici of the piazza.

"This is it," she announced.

Jennifer got out of the car and peered into the piazza. The remains of frescoes decorated each arch and a brick bell-tower towered above. A fountain filled the south end of the rectangular square. Pigeons searched for after-lunch scraps. Vanessa opened the huge mahogany door with a flat-grooved key. Inside the door was a garden and a stairwell that led up into the open air. Vanessa showed her to the first floor, her parents' home. She rang the bell twice and let herself in.

"Mamma. Papa. Hello."

"Si, cara," Mamma's voice sang out. I translate again for you, dear reader. Vanessa's family did not speak any English! And Jennifer understood snippets of their conversation.

Vanessa's mother came into the living room in her slippers and a housedress.

"Mamma, this is Jennifer."

"A pleasure to meet you. We have heard so much. Vanessa says the kindest things about you. Please come in. Would you like a cup of tea? Yes. Good. Some cookies, perhaps. Yes. Good. Vanessa, go dear. Go make your guest some tea. You are an art historian, yes. I wanted Vanessa to pursue art. But she loved books, stories. Always read as a child. She is an editor you know. Has she shown you her work? A fine writer. I wish she would move back home. Even the city of Pavia would be close enough. But Florence, it is another world down there. I hear that is where you met. I hope you were comfortable in the castle—it can get damp there. It was OK? Yes. Did you go out into the gardens? We have won prizes for the rhododendrons. The pink ones. My husband plants them. You are pretty. Your blond hair is unique for Italy. Yes, very pretty. Your husband? He works in a bank I hear. Yes. Works hard. Makes a lot of money, probably. No, not so much? I would have thought more."

Vanessa brought in a pot of tea, some sliced lemon, and brown cookies on a beautiful painted wooden platter.

"Thanks, cara," Mamma smiled.

"Vanessa, your friend is absolutely delightful."

"Yes."

"Has Mamma told you about our store? It's just downstairs. I'll show you later."

"Vanessa." They heard a soprano voice calling through the open window.

"Giovanna, come down. She is here. My sister is dying to meet you, Jennifer. She wants to come visit you in New York if that is OK. I think she is planning to go next spring." As Vanessa spoke, a gorgeous long-limbed skinny creature walked in the front door.

"Benvenuta, Jennifer, to our house. It is a pleasure to finally see you. You are a studiosa. You study art. How marvelous."

This type of awe-inspired conversation went on for at least an hour. Jennifer said very little as the sisters drooled over her looks and apparent intelligence and her New York living situation. The father, arising from his afternoon nap, joined in and they laughed about his trip to New York during which he got stuck in the subway at 42nd Street for an hour and had to cross the tracks on foot to

get out. Visiting the Empire State building was another good one.
Or eating a meal at the World Trade Center. He brought out pictures
of the family trip to Disney World in 1987. Then he dug up the baby
picture album and the beach album and the Paris album, until finally his wife politely asked him to stop before Jennifer passed out.

"Are you hungry?" he asked Jennifer.

"No. Vanessa took me to lunch in Valenza. We had ravioli."

"Yes. They make delicious ravioli in that region of Italy. Better
than in Florence. I can assure you."

"They were good."

"Have you seen our piazza yet?"

"No."

"Toio, she just arrived here. Give her a chance," his wife reminded him.

"Vanessa will give you a tour." He looked at his daughter.
"Vanessa used to love this city. Now she lives in Florence. I don't
know where we went wrong."

"Come on, Papa. We have gone over this many times. I work in
Florence. That is why I am there."

"Yes, yes. Those Toscani. With all their art." Returning his attention to Jennifer, he asked, "And what does your father do? A doctor.
I see. He must be rich. Aren't all doctors rich in America? Yes. I
thought so. I wanted to become a doctor at some point but did not
have family support. They needed me in the store."

That was the first Vanessa had heard her father confess to having
had other aspirations.

"Papa, why didn't you ever tell us?" she said.

"It doesn't really matter anymore. Your mother, does she work?
No. I suppose there really is no reason for her to. No your father
makes a good living. No reason really. They live in Manhattan. The

East Side. Oh yes, my hotel was on the East Side at East 53rd and
Lexington. A nice place, comfortable big rooms. I liked it. Near the
Citicorp building. Is that correct, Jennifer? I thought I remembered
correctly. Tea. Have another cookie."

Vanessa nudged her friend gently on the arm to signal that the
cross-examination would soon be over. They smiled at each other.

"Let me show you the store," Vanessa interrupted.

"Yes," Jennifer got up off the couch.

Vanessa led her friend away from her parents' clutches back
down the stairs out the door and into the piazza.

"Magnificent, really," Jennifer offered before she was whisked
into the furniture store.

"My grandfather opened the shop in 1911, before the war. He
began by selling shoes." Vanessa led her by the beige leather couch
and the chrome and glass coffee table. White ceramic dishes sat
upright on shelves and cut glass twinkled in the store light. They
wound their way through rooms of Persian carpets and marble-
inlayed tables, fold-up couches and reclining chairs, desks and
lamps. It was as if they were on the eighth floor of the Macy's store
in Herald's Square. Vanessa said that her sister Giovanna designed
some of the furniture and that she was very proud of it. They
walked to the front register and took deep breaths.

"Great place," Jennifer commented, slightly wearily.

"Thanks."

They smiled at each other and took a stroll through the city of
Vigevano. They saw the Visconti Castle from the outside and
climbed up inside its cavernous tower. They looked at the church
where many of Vanessa's friends got married. They went into the
biggest bookstore in town and browsed. They had a slice of pizza
and a cappuccino. They walked into the sports store that her friend

Bruno owned and chatted with him. They bought some prosciutto at the delicatessen. They talked about the movies they liked and disliked. They told each other stories about growing up. Jennifer told the one about the time she and her sister put the family cat in the refrigerator and Vanessa the one about her mother's maxi-pad seen crawling down her leg through her panty hose. They laughed together and smiled. It was dark and time for dinner with the family. The flight left early the next morning and Vanessa thought it best that Jennifer get a good night's rest. She needed to get back to Florence that day to begin work. Jennifer's kidnapping was officially over.

I witnessed the following events:

Debbie walked into the ladies' room at Pebble Beach to take a leak. She'd held it in since lunch at Denny's for two hours and ten minutes, according to her calculations, and was thrilled to see that in the downtown area, near the post office, there was a public bathroom, that read Women (figure in skirt) and Men (figure in pants) on two separate doors. As usual, Debbie, a hygienic person, and of Asian ancestry (though she told me later this has nothing to do with why she washes her hands first) walked politely to the sink and washed her hands thoroughly with soap and water. With her lanky 5'8" frame pressed over the sink and her short black hair greased back, she also washed her face. As she was about to walk into a green stall a woman with big gold- and silver-colored hair said to her:

"Are you aware that this is the ladies' room?"

"Yes."

"Let me repeat myself if you didn't get it the first time, this is the LADIES' ROOM."

"I know that." And just as Debbie was about to lock the stall door

behind her a voice rang out. "I get it. You're here to clean it!"
Debbie never did completely recover from that experience, which
incidentally has occurred to even the most buxom and feminine lesbians, and straight women too may I add. There is a group of lesbian women who march in the pride parade every year behind a
banner that reads, "Women Who Are Mistaken For Men In Women's
Bathrooms." Now we need to add, "And Are Asked To Clean
Them."

It is not necessary to describe Jennifer's trip to the airport and
Vanessa's tearful farewell. Suffice it to say that they did not see each
other ever again in this life. They wrote for the first two and half
years. Vanessa dumped Vincenzo. Jennifer started graduate school
at N.Y.U. in graphic design.

Simon prepared himself to meet Jennifer at the airport. He packed
his Walkman and copy of Mark Twain's short stories in his jacket
pocket, an Armani. Black and gray pinstripes would impress
Jennifer, especially with his fresh haircut and matching Armani
cologne. He checked himself one final time in the mirror and
walked out to find a cab. As soon as he raised his hand in the New
York night of about 8:00 P.M., four yellow cabs screeched to a halt at
his feet like a fork scooping up some spaghetti. He chose the one
that did not cut across the entire city block and felt particularly satisfied because if did not smell funky inside. The guy was Jamaican
and smelled good. Wore a clean shirt and was well groomed. The
radio was not blaring but instead moaned subtly.

"Kennedy Airport, please."

"Triboro Bridge OK?"

"Fine."

They did not chat much. Simon got out the requisite $6.00 at the
bridge, priding himself on the fact that he gave the driver the cor-

rect amount before he even needed to ask. He watched Astoria rise
off in the horizon. The elevated train signaled his arrival into this
Greek neighborhood. Then he watched one of the largest cemeteries
in the world appear to his right, home to such greats as Mae West
and others he could not remember. This cemetery in Queens takes
up the space of an entire city, say Versailles, Ohio, and if you were
entering Manhattan from Queens, be it the Midtown Tunnel, the
59th Street Bridge, or the Triboro Bridge, you had to go through it
no matter what and be reminded of your ultimate fate.

Next on Simon's left was La Guardia Airport, one of the ugliest
sights on the face of this earth. Not only were the hangars particularly distasteful, but the summer smell from Flushing Bay was nau-
seating: the sewage from Flushing (the town) pours directly into the
bay. Has been doing it for years, right near the Tasty Bread factory.
The sight of the 1968 World's Fair, whose metallic sphere still stood
despite years of vandalism, made Simon cringe because it seemed
to him to be so lonely and without meaning. Buildings, constructed
edifices of any kind, should have meaning, a purpose, he thought.
Otherwise they ought to be destroyed or replaced. The globe just
stood there, still.

Next was Shea Stadium. Now that was really a joke. After the
Mets' great 1986 season, the stadium had undergone millions of
dollars of restoration, plastered with neon figures hitting baseballs
to hide the original hideous sixties decor. But the Mets were going
nowhere fast again this season, so the decor, which Simon could
better envision in Minnesota than here, was senseless. The Mets
were now the constant subject for David Letterman's nightly show.
They ought to begin by tearing down the stadium and erecting one
outside of Queens. Simon, if you couldn't already tell, despised
Queens, his original home before his father got the hell out of

Elmhurst General Hospital and moved to Newton, Massachusetts. But Simon kept his memories of the Studebaker and the winter night his father took it to the World's Fair globe parking lot and did figure eights on the ice. Queens was where it all began for Simon, and where it all begins for many new immigrants.

The next sight was Jamaica. The row houses were rundown and parks littered with paper and plastic. Many of the roads weren't paved. In the greatest city in the world, some streets are not paved. Simon could tell you exactly where: 245th Street and Conduit (pronounced Condooooit.) He dated a woman there once for six months. Sometimes they had to cross dead bodies to get home. No, not really. It just felt that way with all the garbage piled up on the road. Simon had some stories to tell about that girl. He loved to tell them to his friends. Not to Jennifer. That wouldn't be fair.

The Van Wyck Expressway is the last thing in New York one would miss if one moved away from the city. There was always traffic on this road and three-inch grooves were carved into the pavement, showing decades of neglect. Huge 1960s bombs and smelly trucks crawled on its path. It was completely straight from the intersection with the Grand Central Parkway south to the Southern State, not even a slight curve. Straight as a board, like a road from Willows, California, to Sacramento. Except that in California, you have mountains to look at. Off the Van Wyck was South Queens, a neighborhood you did not want to get lost in. Amidst this desolate place rose the Trump Plaza. This is hard to believe, you tourists, Simon thought, but one of The Donald's first financial ventures was the hideous brick building lining the Van Wyck Expressway. In grimy red lettering his name was proclaimed throughout the land: Trump Plaza.

It was at about this point in the drive that Simon began to smell the jet engine exhaust. He loved that smell. Next to the Stella D'Oro factory in the Bronx (off the Major Deegan Expressway) Kennedy's smell was his favorite. Reminded him of his travels with his family to Paris. Life changed whenever he smelled jet fuel, and his antici-pation for change fed Simon with a burst of energy like that provid-ed by a Three Musketeers bar. He picked up some new people there, he went to a distant land, he went to the airport bar; all signi-fied change. The jet fuel made the grass gray. Signs designating the names of the airlines were gray, too, even though originally red, yel-low, blue, green, and orange.

"British Airways," Simon reminded the driver.

"Yes."

They looped around the airport, through detours and around Hertz Rent-a-Car Grumman buses. The cabby triple-parked, pressed the fare button and waited for Simon to pay.

"May I have a receipt please?"

He tore it off and gave Simon his change.

"Keep three, sir."

"Thanks."

Simon walked through the glass revolving door in search of a flight information screen. Looking up he found a row of screens under signs that read "Arrivals." Anxious parents chased kids beneath them as carts and people pulled by.

"On Time," Simon read with relief.

He walked away for a split second and returned to read the gate. sixteen. A good number. He watched sleepy-eyed travelers scratch their heads. Kids with food on their shirts held their moms' hands, and grannies limped off. A balloon-toting family spotted their rela-tives and screamed with joy. As on the day they met, Simon saw Jennifer, her neck stretched out searching for him in the crowd. He waved. "Over here." Relieved, she recognized his sweet voice. "Simon," she called. Spotted him, dropped her bag, and they embraced for what seemed an eternity.

"I'm so happy you are home."

"I love you Simon."

"I love you, too." The adventure was over for now.

"How was the trip?"

"Fine. Fine."

"The work?"

"Fine. Fine."

"You look great."

"Thanks."

He grabbed her bag and led her out the door, across the street and to the cabstand.

"Simon, I have such an incredible story to tell you."

"Wait till we get in the cab."

They took the next available taxi.

"West 85th and Broadway," Simon said to a new Irish immigrant. "And take the Triboro Bridge."

"Yes sir." Simon hugged Jennifer and said go ahead.

She told the entire story about Vanessa and her family and the castle and then gave him the gold tie clip that she had stored in her purse.

"And look at the ring she bought me."

"I'm really sorry we can't lounge all day," Mary said looking into her lover's eyes.

"Me too."

"Fiammetta, would you like to look at my family album? Do you have time?"

"Of course. I don't have any reason to go back and stew with my family."

Mary gracefully slinked out of the sheets and scampered to the living room. She returned with a plastic colored album, the kind you see at Caldors.

"Here. I've collected these pictures since I was thirteen."

She crawled in bed and laid the album between them.

"That's me and my three sisters, Lisa, Leslie, and Laura. They are all doctors, you know, like my dad."

Fiammetta flipped the page to a head shot of Mary. Her heart stopped. Someone had managed to capture Mary in a pose that made her even more beautiful than Fiammetta had so far experienced. Her icy eyes penetrated by an indirect light caused them to become translucent. She looked right into the camera lens, confident of her appeal.

"Mary, you are magnificent. How old were you in this?"

"Nineteen I think. Yeah. This was one summer vacation back from college. My friend Brenda took it. It's good, isn't it?"

"I'll say." She kissed her hand.

"This is my mom and dad."

"She looks more like your sisters. I think you have your father's good looks. Certainly his eyes."

They took separate showers and met at the door for one last hug. "When will you be back home?"

"Christmas."

Fiammetta was not really used to this type of ending. But realistically their relationship had no future. Her journey went elsewhere.

"I'll write," Fiammetta said.

"I'll respond."

"I'll miss you."

I've tried to make something as true to my heart as possible.